FOREVER TIED

THE FOREVER SERIES

BOOK TWO

AMANDA KIMBERLEY

ABOUT FOREVER TIED

Blood is a bond that ties many unions.

Raine and Skye of the Kersh Witch clan are being hunted by brothers Armand and Alec of the Vlad Vampires clan. And all because Alec blames them for his lover's death in The Were Rebellion.

Alec and his twin brother Armand will stop at nothing to exact revenge for Obsidian, even if it means going back to vanquish the entire Kersh line.

Will both Raine and Skye be able to defeat the Vlads before the brothers end their line? Will they be able to survive and remain forever tied?

Acknowledgments

I want to thank all of my family and friends for your encouragement with this book. You all have a special place in my heart, and we are forever tied.

PROLOGUE
THE WEREWOLF REBELLION

"You can't leave me. We were supposed to do this together." Alec whimpered as he stroked the dark hair of Obsidian Moore. Her perfect porcelain skin was violated with a steady stream of crimson from her forehead. The rounded face and button nose features that wooed him initially to her seemed almost silly to him now, as he stood helpless watching her die in his arms. He wished he could sway the gods to spare her, but shallowness comes with a price, just like any other mortal sin.

It seemed strange to compare himself to the mortals. His brown eyes, chiseled chin, and muscular build made him look every bit as human as a mortal. But his dead heart, the one that hadn't beaten in centuries, made it clear that he was nothing more than a vampire. Damned from the heavens and exiled from the Underworld. He was punished with a sentence far worse than nonexistence. He was dead among the living.

To him, humans had it easy. They possessed free will and could sin as much as they wanted to gain their desires, and it appeared they could do it without consequence. It seemed so effortless for them. It looked like an art.

Sin was something foreign to Alec. He never needed to use it because his wants were always granted. The dark gift made this possible. As a vampire, he could have his material desires met by merely thinking about them. His skills even gave him powers over the humans because their lustful desires made them easy prey.

All the powers he possessed, and all of the material desires on this earth, couldn't help him now. His reason for existence was dying in his arms, and he was powerless to change the course of destiny. His only choice was to watch her die.

Ryback Moore, a witch of the Kersh coven, cast a karma spell upon Alec long before The Were Rebellion had started. The irritant fool thought he could teach Alec how to treat his daughter, a lesson that was now backfiring on them both.

Alec could chant an incantation to the Mother Goddess, trying to disregard Ryback's spell. However, he knew his desire to keep Obsidian on Earth would be met with disapproval. His asking to have her stay, denying her of the soul she should become, would be considered selfish to the Mother Goddess. Even his meager offerings of himself would fall upon the Goddess's deaf ears.

Alec wished it was all a myth. It was honestly unheard of to cast a spell on the undead, and Alec had actually laughed it off at first. Until he discovered what Ryback had done because the Sun God took pity on him and entertained his wishes.

Having no light inside of himself, Alec fell victim to the pact Ryback had made with the Sun God. Thanks to Ryback, Alec could no longer feed upon the humans.

This curse had definite karmic undertones, something humans took as law. Sadly, if Ryback had thought more clearly, and didn't allow his emotions to get the better of him, the spell's bark would not have been worse than the bite. Ryback essentially sentenced his daughter to death by extinguishing her one chance at existence.

"I will always be by your side in spirit," Obsidian said as she palmed Alec's cheek.

"No! You can't die! I won't allow it! You just can't. If I have to, I will find a tribal elder and perform a resurrection spell. You just have to stay. You have no say in this matter." He stated flatly.

Vampires had a selfish nature. They took what they wanted when they wanted it. If that meant keeping someone from the destiny of dying, then so be it. Human law was of no concern to them. He'd do anything he could to keep her here. Existing without her was no existence he wanted to be a part of.

Vampires could not, as humans put it, commit suicide because it was forbidden. Alec could try, but it wouldn't end well. Through legends, he knew a tale of a vampire named Aleister who attempted the same thing.

He purposely stayed up to watch the sunrise. Wanting it all to end because he lost his love. The sun rose, but he didn't feel a singe of burning pain. The gods had apparently, as the legend states, made it snow. The clouds were thick enough that no sunlight could penetrate, causing Aleister to have a fate far worse than nonexistence.

Aleister did die that day. He proclaimed he'd never feel, taste, or touch anything again, and he buried himself deep within the earth. There was talk that he still resides in Transylvania, but it proved only talk. Until now, the story never intrigued Alec enough to seek its validity.

"I must go. The gods are calling me." Obsidian whispered as she loosely gripped Alec's hand.

He could hear her heartbeat fading. The sound was deafening to him. If he didn't know any better, he'd swear his heart was stopping too. He kissed her weak hand. It was pure anguish for him to see her like this.

He had been walking among the living for centuries. A feat few vampires had accomplished. He was respected by many clans. In fact, some of them called him the King of the Vampires. Alec was powerful, and unlike some of his counterparts, he had a hand at magic when his heart was still beating. A practice that made his dark gifts all the more intriguing.

The King of the Vlad Clan was a masterful master magician indeed, bending the elements, slowing time, and could persuade the living to do as he saw fit. He had immense magical powers, but not one of which could heal the dying.

His dark gift, however, could. He could give that gift freely to Obsidian, despite the curse. He was told he'd suffer the worst headache in his life, a small price to pay to keep his love, but there were still no guarantees it would work.

All he had to do was take a taste. Obsidian was so weak that she would not know until it was too late. She wouldn't have time to argue. She'd feel no pain. Her father, Ryback, would still be able to see his daughter alive and well. He could keep her with him for as many selfish reasons as he could dream. He was desperate to keep her all to himself. Any justification would have been a good one to taste her and bestow upon her the dark gift, the blood of immortal life. Any reason, except a pious one.

He had absolutely no right to her. He knew that

because her soul was exceptional. A brighter one than he had ever seen in his dark existence. He couldn't extinguish that light, no matter how much he wanted to. Her soul was just too pure a hue of white to taint it a color any darker. No, she belonged with the gods, and he couldn't deny that.

He gently kissed her hand again and put it to her chest as she took her last Earthly breath. He watched her essence leave the world he was in, and he let out a cry so shrill one would almost think that time momentarily stopped for his grief.

She was gone, and there was nothing he could physically do to bring her back. He was stuck in a world without her and wasn't sure if he could bear it. His breathing felt shallow, which was a bit of a silly notion since his lungs hadn't taken air for centuries. Yet, he could clearly feel an escape of something within him. Something from deep within, a weight on his chest that wouldn't lift.

He couldn't escape the feeling, and it seemed to grow worse. It was now inflicting his vision where he felt a tunnel forming around his corneas. Everything started to blur, and the world turned red like his pupils. His eyes became fixated on one person in the battle.

His rage grew towards Raine, a man he entrusted with his love. It should have been easy for Raine to protect his flesh and blood. He was, after all, Obsidian's cousin. And a powerful man in his own right, the rom baro of the Kersh clan. Standing clad in his black ceremonial robe, he looked determined and focused, trying to defeat the werewolves. But his attention should have been on protecting Obsidian.

Alec wanted to yell and act upon his rage, but he knew better. The werewolves and their rebellion were the top priority, and their feud had to stop. The witches' and vampires' duty was to end this rebellion, which should have never happened in the first place. It was a silly squabble and had nothing to do with Alec's brother Armand or even Armand's heir. The wolves used Kate as an excuse. They caused this rebellion because they felt they were not respected by the vampires.

They were utterly wrong, of course. And what made things worse is that their selfish behavior could throw the entire planet earth out of balance and expose the magical community to the mortals. Their animal instinct clouded their judgment on vanquishing Kate. An open portal wouldn't kill her. It would only make things worse.

The humans could not know of the Underworld or other immortals' existence. It was unnatural and unlawful for that to happen. The humans would attack the immortals out of fear which is why an exposure law was set in the first place.

Particular magical creatures could not readily defend themselves against humans. Sprites, nymphs, and fairies were some of the most vulnerable. If they were injured and unable to continue their magical tasks, an imbalance of nature would occur. And the planet earth would fall out of alignment, causing good and evil to shift. The veil between Earth and the Underworld would lift, freeing the demons. The immortals like Alec that do walk among the living would no longer have the upper hand, giving malignant spirits the ability to over-throw a vampire's power.

It was for this reason, and this reason alone, that Alec's feelings had to be masked from Raine for now. He had no choice. Alec had to wait until there was a proper time to unleash them. His magical gifts allowed him to keep his thoughts to himself, even while in front of Raine, who was a skilled mind reader in his own right. But even though he could block Raine from his own mind, he couldn't stop his own from thinking.

You bastard. She's your blood, unlike that bitch you call a soul mate. I will kill you slowly, but not before I vanquish that shrew right before you. I will rob her of her soul. A befitting fate for you, my brother, indeed.

A faint smile formed on Alec's face as he killed a couple of werewolves with his bare hands. It had been a long time since he had smelled the perme-ating sweetness of blood, and he had ceased hunting anything but vermin while with Obsidian.

Ryback had always thought he had a hand in Alec's sudden change in tastes, but it was Ryback's daughter, and not the spell, that made all the difference. The smell of blood was menial with vermin, and Alec filled his nostrils with as much sweet nectar as he could before it dissipated.

Now that she was gone, nothing was stopping him. His love for existence was slain, ripped out of him, through her lifeless body. He saw little point in holding back because the pain of losing her was far worse than the pain of killing what he deemed as a meaningless mortal.

A werewolf, who was human most of the time, was considered mortal to vampires. However, many vampires felt that werewolves were a distant cry from regular human beings. If a werewolf was a table wine, an average human would be a Domaine Romanée-Conti.

There was always little talk of vampires mistakenly biting a werewolf. Alec assumed they must have tasted vile, but he could never honestly know that. The vampires who made that crucial mistake usually never lived long enough to tell the tale.

The smell of blood was intoxicating, and Alec knew he'd have no problem coming off the wagon again. But this werewolf's blood smelled awfully gamey to Alec. He could only imagine that the taste would be the same. He had never cared to try, but he would make the exception this time.

Mortal virgins were the best to Alec. They would have been his prime choice before the spell. Their blood could be compared to sipping Perrier-Jouet Belle Epoque, the world's finest and most unique champagne. There was no disdain taste to a virgin because they were pure. Tasting them again would be his only enjoyment, and he hoped to find one in this battle soon.

He found another victim. It was a girl this time. He came up from behind her and snapped her right arm back. The sound of crushing bone was music to his dormant ears. His smile grew to more significant proportions as he lowered her body to the ground and tilted his prey's now brittle head back.

As the day turned to dusk, he could see balls of light forming an alignment out of the corner of his eye. Years ago, he would have never paid attention to such a thing. Other immortal's spells and superstitions were of no concern to him. He could exist beyond an Underworld attack, so a planetary alignment sparked little fear in him.

This time was different. And because of Obsidian, he momentarily stopped to look at the sky. He knew she was as dead as his soul, but for a second, he held unto the weakness of a human's hope.

Could her presence still be here? If she were in spirit, could he still have her?

She somehow still held power over his thoughts, even now. He wanted to feel her next to him, and he knew that was impossible. Those thoughts made his anger grow even more.

A tear droplet formed on the skin of his prey. It glistened in sparkles, signifying the beauty of the planetary alignment in the night sky. The beauty of that tear may have also persuaded him to glance up. But the fearful pain behind that drop lost meaning after Obsidian's last breath. The fate of the life between his hands meant nothing to him.

He had never seen a planetary alignment before. The beauty of the balls of light held his attention as he drew his prey closer to his kiss of death. As he bit down, a feeling of ecstasy came over him, and even though he knew it could not be possible, he thought he could feel his own blood rush through his entire body.

The blood quenched his tongue first and then smoothed his throat. As the blood of his prey started to flow, the thirst and desire grew, and he began to gulp. It was a long and welcomed drink and one that didn't cause any pain. He wanted to savor every ounce. It was a drink he had missed for nearly a year, a tiny blip of time for a vampire. However, it was still sadly missed, and his foolishness wanted this kill to last forever as he closed his eyes tight.

He then opened his eyes for a minute, wondering if this could be a dream. The curse should have stopped him from this pleasure, and it clearly was not. Once his eyes got into focus, he noticed Ryback in the distance being thrashed and decapitated by a werewolf.

Alec then knew it was not a dream. Ryback's spell was as dead as he was. A few droplets remained and were still flowing as Alec removed the lifeless body from his mouth. It was sucked dry by his ravish behavior. As he dropped it to the ground, he noticed that her pale features reminded him of Obsidian. His thoughts of her started to race.

The connection to her is still so great. It is as if she were still here. Could she be? No. She was dead.

Overwhelmed with grief, he did something he had never done before. The thought was silly to a vampire but relatively humane for a mortal. He closed the eyes of the prey's lifeless body. He then walked away.

He wondered why thoughts of Obsidian were still plaguing him. She was gone. He saw her take her last breath, yet he could still feel her presence. It was almost as if she were right in front of him.

Alec reached into the air, where he thought he could feel her presence, trying to grasp what little he could sense. It was a foolish thing to do, and he didn't believe in such ludicrous things. But the reaching made the want and need of her tangibility seem more achievable.

He could never reach her, though, and that reality was setting in quickly. He had an eternity to mourn her. An eternity. It was an anguishing concept. There would never be a way of escaping the pain of mourning her. Damned to walk the earth forever, he had no escape or solace from the pain. The only thing he had left was the determination to find pleasure in his miserable existence.

Revenge will be mine for the taking. All I have to do is wait because time is what I have a bountiful lot of.

His thoughts turned again as he looked for his next prey and a white wolf stood before him on the mountaintop. He had never seen a white wolf before. Most of the ones he'd seen were a drab grey or buff-colored tan, and he had even seen a black one. That one went by the name of Keme Freeman.

Keme was special in Alec's eye. He was an old wolf that lived longer than most and thought only about pleasing himself. It was almost as if he was cut from the same cloth as Alec. His color befits his demeanor nicely. The fur on that dog was something Alec could respect. The wolf he could not, but he could appreciate the coat's color.

The white on this one was incredible, though. It piqued Alec's interest in discovering how pure the color truly was. He found desire rising up in his body again. This hunt would be magnificent because nothing would please him more than taint the purity out. A hue of crimson was a perfect shade to slay the immaculateness before him.

Alec lunged forward and leaped off of the rock he was perched on. He outstretched his hands, tingling from the ecstasy of anticipation, and went for the jugular of the white one. The dog turned to look at Alec, anticipating his move, and shot an energy ball his way.

Alec became paralyzed from the blow, but the werewolf's azure eyes made him feel more of a retraction to incapacitate his body. The mere sight of this dog's eyes made him shrivel in his thrill for the hunt. The eyes looked familiar to him, and he tried to place them.

Was Obsidian truly back from the dead?

Alec tried to shake his head but had failed miserably. He was still stunned and could not move, but even if he was not, the thought was impossible. Obsidian was not bitten by a werewolf. She was slain by one of her own—a witch from the Nuri clan. He saw it with his own eyes. There would be no way that this werewolf standing before him was Obsidian. She was dead. And not that long. Even the gods could not force a reincarnation so quickly. No, she was gone.

Another ball of energy overpowered him. He could feel his dead body going limp again. He wondered if this was perhaps what death felt like. Of course, he was not sure. He had never really remembered dying himself. He was made by Lilith, the Queen of the damned, and she was the most powerful vampire to walk among the living and the dead.

She discovered the veil between the two worlds during the times of Adam and Eve. Scorned by her first love, Adam, and her second love, Dracula, she retreated to the darkness of the Underworld with grief, waiting for that one day she could rise again. She found that chance in Alec.

He tried to release his body, give in to the weakness, wishing that act could make him die. Death, though, was something he would never have. Lilith robbed him of that peace long ago because her insatiable love for him sealed his fate.

Lilith, like all vampires, was selfish and did not allow all of her gifts to be passed to Alec. The gift she chose to keep for herself was the ability to walk among the living and the dead. The selfish gesture made him feel like the bastard child, never being or feeling accepted in either realm.

What made it worse was that the gods didn't accept him either. He was born hard to kill, a master of magic and illusion, but doomed to an eternity of death among the living. Armageddon, a day most mortals fear, was a day that could not come soon enough, as far as Alec was concerned. He'd finally get his peace. The gods would absorb his essence, and he would cease to exist.

Lilith was not spared either. She was doomed to live an existence without a mate. Her betrothed, Adam, the first man to ever walk the earth, rejected her. It was indeed a fate far more significant than his at the time. Sadly though, she brought this upon herself. She chose to be petty. And, against the gods' wishes, she sired Alec.

He could never understand it at the time. He was only a fledgling drunk with power, but he now knew exactly how Lilith felt. Losing love was beyond hell, and he could clearly understand her lust for revenge against the gods. He also sympathized with her want of nonexistence. Life was miserable without Obsidian.

A prick to his skin interrupted his morbid thoughts. The fangs from the white wolf dug into his arm. The pierce felt more like a prick rather than a puncture. But for him, it was always hard to tell. The dark gift never made him feel much pain. And becoming powerless from the energy balls was more reason for being unsure. His mind was cloudy, making it hard to comprehend what was happening.

Alec closed his eyes for a few minutes, and when he opened them, he was in a cave. He could hear the sounds of the war still going on outside, but he could do nothing in response. His body still lay limp, and his mind was too dizzy for him to try and attempt to stand.

He did have some sense about him. He knew that this white wolf was not what it seemed to be. It couldn't be because it spared him. If it indeed were a werewolf, it would not have done so.

Werewolves, in general, did not like vampires.

They couldn't understand them. A vampire would never die for their kind, nor would they help a fellow vampire in need. Not unless it suited them.

Werewolves were loyal to the core. They'd do anything, even die for any member of their pack. This difference made it hard for the werewolf to trust a vampire. Vampires weren't completely untrustworthy, however. They would gladly align with other creatures if they saw fit, but that separated the vampire from the werewolf.

A vampire was selfish to the core. They were considered the immortal family's teenagers because they had all the luxuries of mortal life. Gaining worldly possessions, thrills, and anything desired was easy, but it was all behind closed doors. They were loners in the darkness. Some were so good at hiding in the dark that they became famous writers in the mortals' world. There was talk of Edgar Allen Poe being a child of the night, but that had never been confirmed.

Vampires, unlike mortal teens, were not self-centered by nature. They would, on occasion, please a mortal, but only if that pleased them in return. This was primarily due to law and really nothing more. Vampires had a strict set separate from every other creature's codes of conduct. They did this because they felt superior to the other races.

"You should rest, Alec. You will be needed again soon by the clan."

Alec thought he could hear the comment as plainly audible dialogue, but he saw no one in front of him, and the sound did not seem like it was uttered in his ears. He became confused.

"Close your eyes." The voice from nowhere said.

His mind wanted to ponder who this faceless voice could be, but he felt weak and entered darkness again.

"That's it. Let the dark sleep take you into oblivion. We don't need to think about the love lost today. Let's just think about winning the war tomorrow." Whispered Lilith as she grabbed hold of him and dug them both six feet into the ground.

It had been almost 17 years, and they had not seen any sign of him since The Were Rebellion, but that didn't mean that Skye stopped looking over her shoulder. Skye and Raine moved to Savannah, Georgia. It was easier to leave the past that way, especially after losing Obsidian. The mortals' World War also made it easy to pack up and leave everything behind. There was not much left after the soldiers had the pillaging sprees. They found a modest, stead ranch with enough land to live comfortably off. The added crops also brought in a reasonable price in the city.

The days that turned into years were wearing comfortable. Thoughts settled in that perhaps Alec was not coming for them. Life became ordinary, which made Skye feel good.

Each crick and crack of the house instilled a nagging away at the goodness. Skye would close her eyes and try and block out the negative noise, but visions of Raine's demise would soon follow. It was terrifying and left her frozen with fear on her worst days and looking over her shoulder on the good ones. Her visions had been wrong before, especially regarding the paranoia known as Alec. But before him, it wasn't all that often that she was wrong.

She wished with her heart and soul that she could have seen more of the specifics in the vision. A day, or year, would have been nice. It would have made things easier, maybe even more apparent, because if she were sure that this would be their last day, the last kiss they'd share, she would have made sure it was more than just a good morning peck.

The barley was plentiful this year, and she knew he wanted to get a jump start on the day before the heat got to the crop. It would be a long and hungry winter for them if he did not. That jump on the day robbed her of any recollection of her visions from the night before. In fact, the day seemed like any other.

All seemed normal as she was going about her daily duties, and she gave no thought to Alec whatsoever. She even selfishly stole some daydreaming moments of being with Raine in bed that night while cleaning the coop.

After cleaning the coop and collecting the daily eggs, Skye walked to the kitchen to prepare breakfast. She heard a bang. The broom on the opposite end of the kitchen fell to the ground, signifying unwelcome company coming. She quickly reached for the broom in a desperate attempt to cleanse the house, but before she could complete the task, a whirl of misty green light rippled around the kitchen. The light turned into balls and began to form a man's figure.

It was too late because Alec found them, and there was no time to prepare for battle. It was not in Alec's nature to take them as prisoners, and he wanted them and every other Kersh witch to pay for Obsidian's death.

She whispered under her breath, praying that the gods would be forgiving, but she knew better. The outcome of this war between them and the Vlad Clan wouldn't end well.

Alec's fingertips tingled with anticipation as he grabbed the coveted book inside the mountain. Dracula hid it deep in a cave centuries ago. Far before the Americas were discovered. At a time, these mountains were named the Onyx Mountains, and many witches performed spells near the base because it made their spells more powerful. After the Were Rebellion, Dracula hid many of his books to keep them from creatures he deemed evil. A smile dressed Alec's face after he blew the dust off the tattered green leather-bound book.

"Is it really the one?" Armand asked. "Will it give us the spell to destroy their entire coven?"

"Patience, brother! Patience!"

"Obsidian and my Kate are dead because of

them! They deserve a fate worse than death, and this spell seems proper. Don't you think?"

"Yes, it does."

"Brother, I will always be there for you. That connection did not break just because we are children of the night. I still feel your pain and thoughts, and I'm so sorry." Armand said as he touched Alec's shoulders.

"I know," Alec said, smiling. "Let's see."

Alec opened the book to page one and caressed the gilded edges.

"We have finally found the right book. I remember this tracking spell when I was in Dracula's library, gathering the books he wanted to be hidden from us. We just have to find the right page now."

He fumbled through a few dozen pages, came upon the spell he needed, and smiled again.

"Here it is!"

"Do we need anything for it?"

"No. We just need to say it in the right place."

"Not here?"

"No. We need to travel higher up. The map is here. It doesn't seem that far from where we are now. See, we are close to this river." Alec said while pointing to the opposite page of the spell.

"Ah, okay, but can't we try to say this now? Just for practice? It won't take long to get there, and I want to ensure we say it right."

"I suppose. It wouldn't hurt, I guess." Alec said as he grasped Armand's hand.

"In this time and in this hour, we call upon the ancient powers to make time bend and correct mistakes for the gods' sakes."

A cloud of silver mist forms around the two brothers' feet. Surprised by the circling cloud, the brothers released their grasp of one another and tried to escape from the mist, but before they could break free, the smoke encompassed them whole.

Alec closed his eyes. It was the first time as a vampire that he was uncertain about his continued existence.

TWO

BATH ENGLAND 1306

"Hey! Open your eyes. We are fine, thank the gods, not sure where we are fine at, though." Armand said with a nudge to Alec's shoulder.

Alec opened his eyes, and to his dismay, he knew where they were. The spell should not have worked that easily because they did not perform it at the correct time or in the proper place. It apparently worked, however.

"Thank the gods, indeed. Armand, we were granted our wish! We can change the course of history!"

"What do you mean?"

"We were brought back in time. See the scroll on this door? It's dated 1306! That's when Raine's great-grandmother would be born! We are back in England, brother, and if we vanquish her, Raine will not exist, and so, my revenge will be complete!"

A wry smile came over Armand's face as Alec explained everything.

"And a complete revenge you shall have!" Armand said as he placed his hand on Alec's shoulder.

They both started out for the nearby forest to not alarm anyone of Kersh's descent of their presence. As they made it around the side of a large rock, they heard several twigs snap and sensed a distinct earthy scent.

"What do you think that is, Alec? An animal, perhaps?"

"You are still quite the novice, brother, aren't you? It's another vampire. Keep quiet, and I will try and throw off our scent so as not to alert the chap of our presence."

Lilith sensed the two of them from miles away. She was unsure who they were, but they both seemed very familiar. A sense of connectedness overcame her as Lilith took in their faint musky smell. She had not felt this connection in what seemed like forever with anyone except Drake. Dracula was her one true love. And as far as she was concerned, the fling with Demetrese, the ruler of the Underworld, never happened.

This impression was also peculiar because she understood there were very few of her kind around these parts. To sense more than one vampire she experienced as close a connection to as Drake was very out of the ordinary.

Lilith hoped the both of them were friendly, but deep down, she knew that the probability of that was slim. Many gods were upset with her for falling in love with Dracula.

The vampire was well respected by his people because he ruled during peace. Drake was not all that peaceful of a man since he was a vampire. He tended to grant men a violent end if they broke the laws in Transylvania. But that wasn't what the gods faulted her for. She was a goddess as far as the gods were concerned. Sure, she was cast out of Eden, much like Lucifer was cast out from the Otherside. But that didn't make him any less of an angel or her a goddess. So when she fell for a demon, they were furious.

Lilith saw a slight hint of purple in the air next to a rather large rock. She smiled as she realized that one of the two was trying to throw her off their trail. The notion was a little cute but far more amusing than anything else.

Her shoulders lowered, as did her jawline once she was almost upon them. The two clearly had no sense of who she was and seemed more fearful of her than she was now of them. Still, their action was perplexing to her.

Who were these two vampires, and what were they doing in England? I thought only Drake and I escaped to Bath?

The fall of the Roman Empire was the most fantastic excuse to come to England. Drake had taken to eating vermin in Transylvania to avoid hurting his people, but Lilith needed a meatier diet. The rats had made her fall ill. She had become relatively weak and needed to feed off of humans.

Drake was reluctant to allow her to delve into such a diet, especially in his kingdom. If word had gotten out, he would undoubtedly have been overthrown. The townspeople would not think twice about killing his love and setting fire to the castle.

Lilith appreciated that such exposure would eventually lead to their demise. So she convinced him she would only take what she needed and choose her victims from a remote town to avoid suspicion.

A twinge started in the small of her back and traveled up through her shoulders. A sense of coolness overcame her as the realization of exposure set into her bones. She was always careful, but if two more vampires were feeding in the same place, it might make the gods angry.

Lilith needed to get a closer view of these two.

She did not need the humans, or worse, the were-wolves, sanctioned by the gods, to come after her and Drake. Her cold heart loved him too much to try to survive her existence without him.

She had to be cautious of these two since she was unfamiliar with them and their powers. To move any closer might only make them run. Her trajectory power was the best option to see both of them remotely.

The two had to be novices because they should have been able to hide their location a little better from her. Not that they would have gone unnoticed since she was the most powerful of all vampires, but their lack of a better attempt made them appear to be new fledglings.

Lilith closed her eyes and quickly projected herself in front of them. She squinted as she saw the two images look almost identical. The only thing separating the two was a slight difference in the shape of their eyes. Both had dark hair, were muscularly built, and had dimples on their right cheek, making them irresistibly beautiful vampires. But the one with the more circular eyes was most appealing to her, and she did not understand why.

She was drawn to him as if he was her own as if she sired him. And that proved silly because no human deserved her immortal powers, especially a man. After Adam and the gods cast her out, she decided long ago that she would never bestow the

Dark Gift on any human. She wouldn't allow herself to spend eternity with anyone. And not only that, men like Adam did not deserve what she had to offer.

The more exquisite one turned his head and looked out past the rock.

"Whoever it was is gone now."

Lilith pouted at his egotistical statement and then shook her head. Such a pretty boy vampire should know far more than he does. She touched his cheek with her hand to taunt him with her pull, and the vamp's body obeyed her by turning his cheek towards her palm.

"Do you sense that, Armand?"

"What?"

"For a second, I thought that," his voice trailed. "No, it can't be her. Impossible."

"We will get the justice she deserves, Alec. We just have to wait for the child to be born, and then we can avenge Obsidian's death."

"I'm not talking about Obsidian, Armand."

Lilith's eyes widened.

The child? These two would have to be fledglings to speak of such vile things! No vampire is allowed to touch a child. It is an unspoken law for every immortal to abide by.

As they both came to their feet, Lilith thought it was best to follow them in the shadows. A plan of their magnitude should never come to fruition since it would expose all magical creatures to the mortals. The gods would surely destroy these two out of anger, but? Gods were fickle and just might punish all vampires. She wouldn't have that on her conscience. This plan to harm a child would make them angry enough to eradicate the entire vampire race.

Both she and her dearest Drake may cease to exist. She would see that these two were stopped at all costs, even if Lilith had to vanquish them herself.

THREE

"We don't have a choice, sweetness. Alec has decided to walk among the darkness, and he is now our enemy. We will have to vanquish him when the time comes."

"I can't wrap my head around the fact that he wants to hurt us, Raine. It was never in his character to do so. And he took that blood-brother oath with you during the Were Rebellion!"

"None of that matters now, Skye. We have to get to Zhang. You understand it as well as I do. Zhang is our only hope in defeating both Alec and Armand. They are too powerful for us to defeat on our own."

Skye tried to hold back the tears, but they escaped the corners of her eyes and slid down her cheeks.

Raine caught a few with his thumbs as he

cupped her cheeks and pulled her close. Their foreheads met as he whispered, "It will be all okay, somehow. I'm certain of it."

"You don't sound all that convincing," Skye said faintly as her eyes drew away from his.

"I can't lose you, sweetness. You are my forever. You always were, and you always will be throughout time."

He kissed her softly and then buried his head in her chest. "Promise me something?" he said in an almost inaudible tone. "Please don't ever leave me. I don't think I could handle life without you."

She held his head and raised it to make eye contact with hers. Skye looked into his dark eyes sincerely, desperately hoping hers would soothe them, but she recognized they would not. There were too many uncertainties. First, there was Alec and Armand. And second, there were the gods and one demon to consider. Thanks to Demetrese, Skye and Raine were no longer immortal. So now that they had to reincarnate to be together, both the gods and Demetrese, the ruler of the Underworld, cast free will upon humans. Thanks to that power, they had to freely fall in love with one another every lifetime.

The only thing that remained constant was their love for each other, and somehow she had to convince him that her love would be enough. He was asking for an almost impossible task. They only narrowly made it through the Were Rebellion alive. And now, he wanted her to promise they would survive Alec and Armand's revenge. She may never be sure of that, but still, she somehow, deep down, felt confident enough to give him the answer he was seeking. "I promise we are forever tied to each other, my darling."

Was it the gods that made saying this so easy?

She found it hard not to wonder.

I t was not a long wagon ride to get to Zhang's cottage. He settled on land surrounded by a forest and close to the healing powers of a hot spring in Colorado.

His cottage was in a remote enough area where he would remain undetected from the Crows, a known tribe of natives that now hated the magical community.

The Crow believed witches, sorcerers, and even vampires, brought upon the destruction of their land and their tribal leaders. Despite all the Kersh clan protests, the Crows never included the werewolves in the blame. In fact, the Crow believed the werewolves were an asset to their tribe. Keme became their alpha and hunted for the mortals.

This made things hard for the witches because

Keme was another sworn enemy. Raine and Skye's only solace was that Keme would never kill a human, and now that witches were mortal, he couldn't hurt them.

But animosity grew after the Were Rebellion between the tribe and the clan. This made it hard for the magical community to protect the mortals from the real threats of demons, rouge weres, and vampires.

Zhang, a powerful and neutral sorcerer, had found solace in the hot springs after the magical community's fourteenth-century peace treaty was drafted. Zhang yielded its healing powers so the balance between good and evil would return to normal. It was the best thing to do given the circumstances, and he hoped that the sting of betrayal the magical community felt towards Alec and Armand would someday fade in the centuries to come.

"It's nice to see you again, old man," Raine said as he slowed the horses down. He unhitched them from the wagon so they could drink from the springs.

"Who are you calling old?"

"Fair enough!" Raine said with a chuckle.

"Skye, it is nice to see you too. I hope this meeting is under better circumstances?"

"No, I'm afraid not, Zhang. I've had a vision that Alec and Armand are after us again. We were both hoping you might help us."

"I can, Skye. Come! We have much to gather before the sun goes down." Zhang patted them both on the shoulders and led them to his garden, where he pulled up some beets and potatoes. He motioned Skye to pick sprigs of basil, lemongrass, parsley, and thyme. Skye plucked them with a perplexed look.

"The beets and potatoes are for the stew. I'm sure you both are just as hungry as I am! The herbs are for the spell working we will do tonight. Sounds like you have a small block. These will give your psychic powers the boost you need once I smudge you."

Night had fallen quickly after they all ate. Zhang started a fire in a pit he had made just outside the home. Skye was pleased that he did because it was just the cure she needed for the chill she felt in the air. She crossed her arms desperately, attempting to dissipate the bumps forming on her skin while real- izing it was odd for her to be cold so close to the hot springs.

The chill started moving from her shoulders, traveling to her neck and down her spine. Skye shiv- ered again.

"That's no breeze. What are you sensing, sweetness?"

"I'm not sure, but it's not good. The brothers have a plan already—don't they, Zhang?"

"I cannot be truly certain, but from what I can

read off of your aura, it appears so. Let me finish bundling the herbs."

Skye sat by the fire as she watched Zhang bundle the herbs. He asked her to stand as he wafted the now billowing sweet fragrance with an eagle's feather all around her body.

He started with her head, and Skye noticed the breeze from the feather tickle the nape of her neck, causing the tiny hairs to rise. The sensation made her shiver down to her toes.

As Zhang slowly moved from her neck towards her shoulders and the middle of her back, she realized that the hairs on her neck weren't rising due to Zhang.

Tiny balls of silver blue lights swirled before her like a colony of fireflies and formed into a human-like figure. Skye immediately recognized the form as the Indian goddess Durga.

"Brightest Blessings, my dear daughter! Your friends will not hear me because they are not my daughters."

"Will they see you?" Skye blurted out before realizing she was audible to Raine and Zhang.

"Yes, they will be able to see me," Durga said as she waved her hand in front of the dancing lights.

"Skye? Do you see what I see?"

"Yes, Raine, I do."

"She must be here to give us some news. I'm sure it will have to do with the twins." Said Zhang.

"The twins have traveled back in time, my darling daughter, and it is not good. They plan to end the Kersh line before it starts. They want to kill Raine's great-grandmother before she's ever born. But? Their plans are being thwarted. They cannot change the course of history, which is why Lilith plans to stop them. They were only sent back in time to observe. Once Alec understands what the gods want, he will be forced back to the present."

A smile found Skye's face as Durga reassured her that the brothers would be forced back to this time.

"However, this does not mean that you are completely safe, my daughter. On the contrary, you will be forced to travel with Raine to escape from the twins for the next two decades. I will warn you of their coming once you reach Kentucky, and it is only then that you will be forced to fight them."

"Durga, I do not understand. I thought we wouldn't have to vanquish them. I thought it was written in the prophecies that the King of the Vlads would unite the witch and vampire clans."

"I understand that not all is clear to you, but in time it will be. For now, this is what you need. I must go."

"But Durga?"

The lights that made the goddess appear were now surrounding her again. Skye tried to blink through the brightness, but Durga disappeared when her eyes opened again.

"What did she say?" Zhang asked.

"She told me what we feared the most. Alec and Armand must be stopped."

"I so hoped it would not have to come to this," Raine said.

Alec was surprised to see the date staring back at him on the ledger he signed for the inn they had decided upon.

The year was not too shocking because he learned all about his new enemy's lineage. Raine's great-grandmother was about to be born, and she was the first to marry into the Kersh witch clan. This woman would not only have a hand in raising Raine as the Rom Baro he would become for his people, but she'd also introduce him to Skye.

The day is what shocked Alec the most. He had no idea that Raine's great-grandmother shared the same mortal birthday as both he and Armand. Alec wondered why he had such a strong connection to Raine in the past, and he now realized it was because of the great-grandmother.

Most of the mortals believed that fate was a silly

coincidence. They did not see a connection between numbers and people, but the pull was there. And that was why their blood-brother oath worked during the Were Rebellion.

"That pull may pose a problem, Alec. If it is strong enough, we may be unable to vanquish the great-grandmother alone. What should we do?"

"We will think of something when the time comes, but for now, let's find the mother-to-be's dwelling."

Alec used his senses to track the woman. But when he started, his senses came across another familiar feeling that he found hard to shake. Lilith, his sire, was close.

"Armand, we have to go. Lilith is here. We can't risk her finding us. If we come in contact with her, the spell will be broken and force us back to our time."

"How is she here?"

"That is not important right now. What is important is getting away from Lilith. She cannot be alerted to our presence. Hopefully, our link to her isn't as strong since she has not sired me yet."

"That bond is powerful in our time. How are we going to lose her?"

"By staying close to the shore. I'm hoping her powers will weaken, as other vampires do by the water."

"She is the Queen of the Damned. Those rules may not apply to her, but one can hope."

"Our bond is not formed for another half century or so. There is still a good chance we will be undetected. Come! Let us go before she sees us!"

Sleep came to Skye quickly that evening. This was the first time she was not wholly consumed with tossing and turning. She had Zhang to thank for the comfort of sleeping until a brisk northern breeze awoke her from a deep sleep. But they left Zhang ages ago and were on the run toward Kentucky as Durga wanted.

She lay still and prayed tonight would be different, where she'd escape the nightmares. But as the pictures started to form in her head, she realized that her prayers had gone unanswered again. There was now no denying the horror any longer. Alec and Armand would come for them, and soon.

Morning broke, and Skye fitted herself in a light blue bonnet and matching long, flowing country dress. She started to gather what little they had in her hands. A pot, pan, and hairbrush were the first she grabbed as she ran out towards the wagon.

"There isn't much time. Do we have anything else that is of importance?" Raine asked Skye.

"Only the chickens are left, but you would rather leave them to our neighbors, right?"

It was one of the many homesteads they stayed in on their journey from Colorado to Kentucky. If it weren't for the Kersh Clan, they wouldn't have been able to travel such a distance.

"The Lees been kind, and we cannot travel with them because they'd only slow us down. That'd leave the twins time to catch up to us. We can't risk it."

"I realize that, but our finances can't handle another quick move like this either. Promise me that we will stay longer at the next place?"

"You know I can't promise you that, sweetness."

"What about that spell we did a while back when Alec found us in Iowa? You cast a sacred circle around the altar by the barn with that one. Can't that be expounded upon at the next place?" She asked as she lowered her head and hopped into the wagon.

"We cast that with most of the Kersh clan behind it. That was an awful lot of power, and they could still break through. I don't think you and I are strong enough to hold them off on our own. We narrowly escaped the last time from their grasp. I almost lost you, and I don't think I can find a way to go on without," his voice started to trail off as he was giving the reins a tug.

Skye lowered her head and did not say another word on the subject. Her fear of losing him was as great as his, and tears were sure to follow if they talked about the brothers any longer.

They left yet another homestead behind, and Skye was finding it hard to keep track of exactly how many it had been in the almost 20 years following the Were Rebellion. The first was in Nebraska, the second had been Kansas, and then Iowa was the third, but all the rest were too much of a blur. The only certainty she had was that they would be adding Missouri to the increasing list.

They seemed to be averaging a new homestead every summer to run from her nightmares of Alec, the King of the Vlads, and his brother, Armand. Skye hated to leave Missouri. It was the first place she wanted to call home since The Were Rebellion and leaving Zhang in Colorado.

Obsidian, who was Raine's cousin and Alec's lover, perished during that battle. Neither Skye nor Raine possessed the power to stop it from happening. And they would have done anything to spare her life. Alec should have understood that. Instead, he blamed them for her death. Since then, he vowed to vanquish them and their entire family coven.

Skye hated the nightmares that consumed her.

But those terrors were far easier to handle than the constant reoccurring nightmare of losing Obsidian.

Amid that battle, it was hard to focus on anything else but the enemy in front of you. Skye's attention was held by the werewolf Draven, and she succeeded in getting Draven off of Ryback, Obsidian's father. However, that put Skye as Draven's immediate target. Draven lunged for Skye, and that's when she hit a rock. Once she came to and was dislocating Draven's shoulder, it had happened. The memory of seeing it is forever etched in her brain, even after almost two decades.

Skye had no intention of having anyone die that day. She thought Alec understood that because Obsidian was just as much her kin as she was to Raine. And once Zhang foretold the prophecy of how they'd all continue the legacy of the Kersh Clan, it became clear that the future of their families needed to be protected at all costs. Obsidian was pregnant with Alec's child. The gods granted this because they knew something none of us did then. Ryback would have no choice but to take Alec into the fold because it was Alec and Obsidian's destiny to mend the broken bond between vampires and witches. This child would have been born as both. The werewolves perverted this union, stating it went against everything. Mixing of races, unless it was a werewolf mating with a witch, was forbidden. And those happy prophetic dreams were vanquished the day

Skye saw Obsidian die at the hands of a werewitch of Strega descent.

Skye did know the werewitch's name that killed Obsidian. She only understood him to be rouge. And the rouge bastard gave Obsidian lacerations so deep that Skye and Ryback could not heal her with their magic. Ryback and Skye were many things to the Kersh people, but neither had the power to awaken the dead. The gods took Obsidian for their own selfish reasons, and this was something all of the clan accepted except for Alec.

"Where do you think we should head this time?" Skye found herself asking to try to break the deadly silence between them.

"Kentucky."

"Oh," Skye said, lowering her head even more. It was the last place on earth that she wanted Raine to head towards.

"There are a lot of caves in Kentucky where we can hide. It's getting harder, Skye. I'm not the young man I once was. I'm growing tired of hiding, and this may give us a chance to stay there a little longer like you had wished, but we have to be careful."

"I understand. I just wish that the gods' bidding didn't come with so much recourse."

Raine's gaze was now on her.

"We can't risk exposure. You know it could mean death to the entire clan, sweetness. Not to mention our duty—"

"To hunt the ones risking the well-being of the mortals and magical races. I know. Durga made that so clear when we were with Zhang. But since when does doing the right thing mean we have to constantly uproot our lives? Does Durga enjoy seeing our unhappiness?"

"Yes, it seems those bastards get quite the kick out of our misery," Raine said.

"It's not funny that our unhappiness pleases them so much that they make it a sport! And I, for one, am tired of it! You must promise me more than a year this time, Raine. I can't keep this up, either. I'm getting too old for this too."

"So you'd rather they find us? You want me to watch you die? Is that it?"

"No, of course not! Raine, I didn't mean—"Her voice trailed as she swallowed hard. She loved him with all of her heart, and the last thing she wanted to do was raise her voice at the one person on her side. Her weariness and frustration from constantly running were getting the best of her tongue. And the words of goddess Durga didn't help matters either.

"I get that you didn't mean to upset me, sweetness. But it's my duty to protect you; this is the only way I know how."

"Why can't we just face them?"

"Because Durga told us to wait for her guidance. And because I can't breathe without you by my side, darling." He said as his voice cracked.

"But Durga hasn't shown herself yet. Perhaps our fate has changed?" Skye asked, hoping the words she uttered would make it true.

Raine turned away from Skye, clicked his teeth, and pulled on the horses' reins. It was the first time he ever showed any kind of stoic emotion about Alec and Armand toward her. He did not have to say anything, though. Because the look on his face showed how much her words stung him.

"I'm sorry." She said as she swallowed hard again and smoothed out her dress. "Let's go to Kentucky, my darling, and we will make a house a home there for as long as we can." She knew what she said was flat and would never make up for her foolish banter, but she had to try.

"Skye, please understand that I can't lose you. Ever. We aren't ready to face them. We just aren't. I'm taking us to Kentucky so we can train."

"Okay."

They said very little to each other until they set up camp. Only then did they relax with each other.

"Sweetness, promise me something?" He said as he palmed her cheek.

"What?"

He held her in his arms and brought her close to his chest. Tiny bumps littered her skin as he breathed onto her neck. Her ear bent towards his as he whispered.

"Please don't ever die because I can't breathe

without you."

His voice was almost inaudible as she watched tears forming in the corner of his eyes. She caught them as they slid slowly down his cheeks.

Since they started running, she found it hard to give him any words of comfort. This time she needed to dig deep because she couldn't bear tarnishing Raine's beautiful face with any more sorrow. Her voice remained silent as she held him close, catching every tear he shed for her, Obsidian, and their life before the rebellion.

She kissed his cheek, hoping that small gesture would take away the hurt, and then out of exhaustion, they both found themselves drifting off to sleep in each other's arms. It was the first time in forever that they both slept through the night in shared peace.

The following day Skye awoke first. It was strange to her to be up before him. They usually both awoke together to the sound of their rooster. It was still very early. The sun only started to peek over the horizon. She sat up and watched the day come alive with the sun's warmth and the birds chirping.

Raine rustled beside her as she stretched the

ache out of her muscles.

"Morning, sweetness," Raine kissed her cheek.

"Morning, my dear. Did you sleep as well as I did?"

"I always sleep well with you by my side." He said with a wink.

His words cut through her, piercing her chest and twisting her insides. She reached out for him with trembling fingers. Her right arm pulsated as she sucked in a breath. She had another vision and tried to steady herself with her left hand. Pushing it deep into the ground between them and hoping the gods would be kinder to her weary body with their message.

She drew a pentagram into the earth in an attempt to shield herself from seeing the frightening flashes forming in her head. The pentagram only intensified the vision when the goddess Durga appeared in front of her. Skye shut her eyes tight to block the goddess's appearance, but that proved futile.

Durga showed her different variations of visions, but all the outcomes were the same because they all led to their demise. Skye clenched her heart, which was compressed with a heaviness she had never experienced in all her life. Bile formed in her mouth, and she gagged once her heart reached her stomach.

It had been almost two decades, and Skye

thought that maybe Durga's would not come to fruition. It was a silly notion, but the lapse of time made the vision of Kentucky seem distant.

As Durga continued to speak in images, Skye realized that she could not show her feelings on her face. She couldn't let Raine see her distress from watching him die at the hands of Alec.

"You must not tell him what you are seeing, Skye. The prophecy must come to fruition, which must happen in Kentucky."

This curse of seeing things she had little control over was ripping Skye from her insides. She lay helpless, watching Durga's future events unfold in her mind, and every one of them led to the same outcome. She'd lose the only thing that mattered in her lifetimes on earth.

How can I watch him die? How on earth is this fair to me?

The pit of her stomach reached a new bottom. She desperately wanted to clutch the pain and wish it away. But if she attempted such an action, Raine would see the despair, leading him to ask for a translation of the visions.

Durga was firm that Skye mustn't share this vision with him. Skye turned away and looked at the horizon, hoping to find an answer in the rising sun, but all it brought was the uncertainty of this new day. The day that would lead them to Kentucky and their untimely deaths.

Raine put his hand on her shoulder, and she breathed. She'd have to keep all of this from him, and she couldn't decide what would kill her more. The fact that a goddess was making her keep this from him. Or that she will lose him at the hands of Alec.

"I'm glad. I sleep well with you by my side too." She squeezed out in between the horrid images still plaguing her mind. She then concealed her torment from him by drawing his lips to hers.

Using her wiles was never something she did. They were always open and truthful to each other so concealing her feelings from him was utterly foreign to her.

She frowned, displeased at the gods who saw fit for her to lie to her husband, her soul mate. She tightened a fist at her fears that this would probably not be the last time she would have to keep something from him. Skye buried her face within his broad shoulders and wondered if they would ever allow her to tell him the complete truth again.

"Ready for another day on the road, sweetness?" He said as he broke their embrace.

"Yes."

Skye got up and gathered the pot that was by the fire pit. The smoldering ash reminded her of one of the visions of Alec burning Raine at the stake while Skye was forced to watch. She shook her head to get the awful image out and then used her powers to plant her footing firmly into the earth to garner as much strength as the goddess Durga would allow her. Her feet felt heavy and sank with each step she made toward the wagon. Raine helped her in her seat and kissed her cheek before making a clicking sound with his tongue to get the horses to move forward.

They rode for quite some time, making small talk about the people and animals they came across during their journey until Raine slowed the horses at a lake to take a drink.

"We'll camp here for tonight. This should be the last night before settling in Kentucky."

"Okay," Skye said.

It was the most she could muster. She gazed passed Raine and looked at the countryside. There were a lot of farms garnishing apple trees and grape vines. The scenery was almost peaceful, with Raine constantly leading them to yet another body of water in their search for another new home. Nothing had really caught her eye.

It should not have meant that much, but it did. It was there that Skye lost what she knew as her genuine grip on life. Durga had told her in the vision to rinse everything that mattered to her into the water. That meant little at the time, but now? Everything seemed clear.

Skye looked towards the lake and watched the caps of white swirl and bounce as she took a deep breath. She wanted to please Durga but couldn't release everything she held dear. This request was too hard to do for any mortal.

How can my union with my soul, my only reason for breathing, be rinsed away as if he did not matter?

Her heart compressed with an ache so deep that she thought her chest would explode. Sadly, she knew the pain would haunt her until Alec ended her suffering, and for the first time in her existence, she wanted him to end it.

She tried to smile as Raine touched her shoulder by the campfire. His smile was deep enough to rock her to her core. As he started to kiss her that evening, her thoughts of their deadly future melted away and were replaced by the present she was in. She relished each kiss and caress from him as if it was the last she would ever receive.

A cold tingle rushed through her before her head took refuge in the crux between his neck and collarbone. His loving presence had always made her safe, but this time she knew he couldn't keep that promise if fate ruled their future.

"What's wrong?" She heard him asking.

"It's nothing. The breeze just gave me a chill." She said, trying to reassure him as she kissed his lips, neck, and chest.

She quickly unbuttoned his shirt, exposing his chest to the moon's light, and traced her fingers over the sparse hairs on his chest. Skye then removed his pants and knickers.

His body stood gorgeous, clad in the moon's light, and she couldn't help but gaze upon its magnificence and smile. He cupped her face and drew her lips to his. The soft welcome of them made her melt into his rock-hard chest.

Her stomach quivered as he rested his hands on her shoulders and slid her dress down towards her forearms to expose her cleavage. His gaze hungrily shifted from her eyes towards her bosom. He took a long breath as he cupped her breast and brushed his lips over her chest.

Skye wanted to moan, but she could hardly catch her breath before she realized that he had tugged on her dress enough to completely expose her chest. He let out a breath before his lips glided over each nipple.

Skye finally found her voice and let out a soft moan while she laced her fingers in his hair to pull him closer to her.

"Take me." She said in a whisper.

He took each mound into his mouth and teased the nipples with his tongue. His left hand slid down toward Skye's waist, and as he pulled her closer, she felt his cock press hard against her inner thigh. "Take me. Please, Raine?"

He slid her dress off and guided her toward the ground before plunging his cock into her slick center. Skye arched her back in response, allowing him to go deeper inside her. The sensation made him thrust faster, harder until he shifted his position. Skye let out a sigh of disapproval.

"Not so fast!" He said while touching her lips with his forefinger.

His lips kissed her chest first and then trailed down towards her stomach before gliding down her thighs. His tongue slicked across her clit three times before a moan escaped Skye's lips. Skye tried to catch her breath again but failed.

His tongue continued to circle her clit until Skye writhed beneath him.

"Baby, I need--" Her breath was ragged, shallow.

"I've got you, sweetness. I've got you."

"I need you inside me, and you are not playing fair."

"I never said I would play fair once you gave me permission." He said with a grin and then kissed her neck. "But if you insist, I'll play a little nicer."

He then thrust his length inside of her. Skye tried to explore every inch of him as she pushed back.

Raine moaned, rocking in unison until they both released together.

"I like it when you play nice," Skye said with a chuckle.

The two held each other, and sleep overcame them within a few minutes.

Alec tried as much as he could to free himself and Armand from Lilith's hold. She hadn't made herself known in the woods, but he knew she was following them in the shadows, waiting for a good time to strike.

"I still feel her around us, Alec."

"So do I. I almost want to call Lilith out at this point. It's just useless to keep trying to run from her."

"Agreed."

"Lilith! I know you are following us in the shadows. Show yourself to us." Alec said.

His voice was thick with as much conviction. The Lilith of his time was a bitter and cold shrew, and he imagined that the one in this time was just as ruthless.

Lilith's eyes widened at the novice's words. Even

the eldest of vampires had difficulty with being aware of her presence. So who was this vampire? And how could he hold so much power?

"I am running out of patience, woman! Show yourself!"

Lilith's eyes narrowed as she clenched her hands and formed fists.

"How dare you call me of all vampires out!" Her eyes reddened as she appeared before him before continuing.

"Just who in the mortal's hell do you think you are? I am your queen! You do not call me out as a commoner like yourself! Bow before royalty, you insolent fool!"

Alec had to call her out, but now that he saw the anger seething in her eyes, he wondered if pissing her off was a good idea.

"My queen," Alec started as he bowed, "I did not think it was you. I would not have addressed you in such an offensive way if I did. Forgive my brother and me."

"Well, that is all right, I guess, just as long as it does not happen again. Now then, just what are you two doing here? I am not familiar with either of you. Are you foreigners?"

"Yes, we are, my queen. We come from a place that has many mortal savages. It is quite far from here." Armand said in a nervous tone.

"I see. Does this mean that the one that sired is a

savage too? Certainly must be if you took that tone with me."

"Oh no, my queen! She is not savage at all, but she is very secretive. We were told not to utter her name to anyone."

Alec swallowed hard.

"Hmm, that is a little strange. Most vampires are proud of their fledglings. They would not hide behind them. Who is this vampire, and does she not understand common vampiric law? As the queen, I am made aware of the existence of every fledgling ever made, especially if the fledgling was not made from the Vlad lineage."

"She goes by the name of Chepi."

Alec blurted out the name before he could think properly. He did not want to utter such a familiar name from his time. But Alec was pretty confident that Chepi or her ancestors in the Sauk tribe were not born yet. He hoped that uttering such a name would throw Lilith off, and she'd change the subject.

"I see and can now understand why she wants to have anonymity. A name such as that would bring uncertainty to her doorstep. It sounds savage. You should tell your sire that she should consider renaming herself. A good English name would do her some good."

"I will pass that along to her. We must be going, your highness. May we bid you farewell?"

Alec swallowed hard again. He should not have

asked for her permission, but his manners had gotten the best of him.

"Not yet. I'd like you to state your business here in Bath, England. Seems strange that you would come this far for just a stroll. And if you plan on feeding here, it is my business. Only I and one other vampire reside in Bath, England. We are trying to remain discreet. With you both here, it will become rather difficult to maintain such discreetness."

"We have come to see some old kin. We hear our cousin is with child." Alec found himself saying this little too freely to Lilith. The damned woman still possessed a pull with him, even though she wouldn't sire him for about another half century."

Lilith smiled at him with a toothy grin. It was as if she knew her power of persuasion was working on Alec, and he couldn't help but wonder if his mentioning the child was her doing. If she continued to make idol chat, she eventually would find out their plans. Therefore, he had to try and cut this conversation short.

"Oh? Why would two vampires want to be around old kin? We say goodbye to our mortal lives once we are born into darkness. Didn't Chepi teach you that?"

Alec found he could not keep the truth from Lilith. She was more than a sire to him. She had once filled the void Obsidian left on him once leaving this plane of existence. He may not have found true happiness, but his life with Lilith was more than tolerable. And dare he say enjoyable. To keep his thoughts and feelings from Lilith felt like a betrayal. He tried to search for the right words in his brother's eyes.

"We find it hard to break free from our loss since we are fledglings," Armand stated as an answer for Alec.

"Really? I would think it would be easier for the two of you since it is obvious that you have each other. You were born identical twins in your human life--were you not? I may be the queen of the Damned and understand very little about the lives of mortals since I was never one. Still, I know that your remarkable resemblance to each other means that you were mortal twins. Your sire certainly did the vampire race a service to grant us two beautiful creatures such as yourselves. The power of twins is something we should harness together. Do see to it that Chepi pays me a visit. I insist that you join the Vlad Clan."

"Oh, we will let her know. Now, your highness, we must be going." Alec said with a bow.

"Nonsense! If you are fledglings and so far from your sire, I must help you both with your, shall we say, problem of letting go of your mortal lives. I'd be happy to escort you to your old kin and see that you bid her a proper farewell. Many who find it hard to detach say they are going on a long trip rather than allow their loving mortals to mourn a body they will never find."

"But we can't ask that of you, my queen," Armand stated.

"You do not have to. It will be my pleasure to help."

Lilith led them from the dense forest. She knew her powers would only allow her so much leeway. To have them escort her to the pregnant woman would be the option of the least resistance. They would not be able to kill the mortal child, nor would they be able to turn the babe in her presence, and if they chose to defy her now, she would not think twice about destroying them both.

"Very well. Our cousin is in Portsmouth." Alec said.

"What are you doing, brother? She will ruin all of our plans!" Armand spat in a whisper.

"What else would you have me do?"

"We have to find a way to get rid of her before we make it to Portsmouth!"

"Armand, that is not a wise decision. The best we can do is get her to trust us so we can go along with our plans."

"Very well," Armand said with a sigh.

Lilith smiled at their feeble attempt to hide their conversation from her. She wasn't sure why they bothered to try. A vampire has better hearing than a dog. But, nonetheless, they agreed to have her accompany them. It did not take them long to get to Portsmouth from the English Channel. Lilith knocked on the flat's door, and a woman answered.

"May I help you?"

"Hello, we are here to see Beatrice. We are kin." Alec stated.

A loud scream from the other end of the door pierced their ears.

"Now is not such a good time. Beatrice is with child, and I'm afraid she just went into labor. I must tend to her."

"Perhaps we can help?" Alec persisted as he held onto the closing door.

"All right then, but please, keep out of the midwives' way."

"Yes, Ma'am."

The woman opened the door widely to allow Alec, Armand, and Lilith in and then quickly ran towards a woman who was being helped into a bed.

Alec gathered this woman to be Beatrice herself. Alec's knees buckled once the candlelight danced upon Beatrice's face. She had pure porcelain skin, long dark hair, and dark eyes. Alec sucked in his breath.

"I swear, brother, if I didn't know any better, I'd think I was looking into the eyes of Obsidian's ghost."

"The likeness is so striking, Alec, indeed!"

Alec kept taking shallow breaths as he witnessed the birth progress.

"Sir, since I heard you say you were kin, would you please get the lady some water?" a midwife uttered to Alec.

"Certainly!" Alec said, still in complete shock.

Alec walked to the well directly outside the flat and drew some water as quickly as possible. He did not want to miss even a second of Beatrice's beautiful resemblance to Obsidian. He returned to the flat with the bucket. A midwife quickly took it from him and placed the child in his hands.

"I need you to hold her while I prepare the bath." The midwife said.

The baby opened her eyes, met Alec's gaze, and started crying. Alec cradled the baby as best as he could in his arms. Mesmerized by its beauty. He hadn't had the joy of having his own baby. That pleasure was robbed from him by the Were Rebellion.

"There now, you will be warmer and cleaner soon. All will be righted." Alec said with a beaming smile. He touched the baby's cheek, and the baby's lips nuzzled his index fingertip. "Oh my, you are a hungry one, aren't you?"

The midwife preparing the bath almost instantly took the baby from Alec's hands to bathe her. Alec relinquished his arms to his side and looked at Armand.

"You cannot do what you came here for, can you?" Lilith stated coldly.

"What are you accusing us of?" Armand demanded.

"If I were you, I would not use that tone with royalty, *sir*." She clucked towards Armand.

She then turned towards Alec, "I asked you a question and expect you to answer it. Tell me your intentions with this child!" She spat in a loud whisper.

"I have no intentions. You were right, my queen. I should have said my goodbyes long before this." Alec turned towards Beatrice. "You have a beautiful girl, Beatrice, and may God bless the both of you."

"Why, thank you, sir. I hear you are kin? A distant cousin, I presume?"

"Yes. On your mother's side."

"Your name, sir?"

"Alec."

"That is a good name! I shall call my baby Alexandra, after you, my kin. Thank you for visiting on such a joyous day and caring for my child and me."

Alec swallowed hard and nodded.

"We must be going now. It was a pleasure to

meet kin." Alec said as he turned to the door. Beatrice said goodbye as he set foot on the doorstep. Armand and Lilith followed him.

"What do you think you are doing?" Armand asked. "You know why we are here."

"That is enough, Armand."

"I will ask again, and if I do not find your answer sufficient, I will not be so patient with either of you this time. What are your intentions for being here? You dress differently, which is strange in and of itself. You did not know who I was. You clearly are not from here because you do not understand the law and are unaccompanied by your sire. Be careful with your words because any wrong answer is punishable by death."

"You are right, my queen. We are not from here, and we are unfamiliar with the law. We have no intention of harming any mortal, least of all that child. All we wanted to do was right a wrong." Alec said, hoping this would be enough to suffice his future lover.

A white mist started to form around Alec and Armand. The smoke turned into a thick fog that separated them from Lilith. When the fog lifted, Lilith was no longer in front of them, and neither was Beatrice's flat. They were, instead, surrounded by stalactites.

"Why are we back home?" Armand asked.

"Because we were not there to end Raine's

lineage. We were there for some other reason. Damn you, gods!" Alec said with clenched fists.

"We will find another way, brother."

"The only other way is to exact my revenge on the one person to blame. Let's go find Raine!"

SEVEN

MAY 23, 1553 THE MOUNTAINS IN KENTUCKY, USA

They made a reasonable time after leaving camp. Skye was still smiling from their evening together.

"You look beautiful this morning, sweetness. Such a gorgeous glow on your face."

"Thank you, Raine."

"We will head into town first to get supplies and then head towards the mountains."

Raine pulled the wagon up to the sawmill in town and hitched the horses.

"I'm going to collect some wood. Why don't you go into the mercantile and see what food they might have for supper?" Raine said as he outstretched his hand to help Skye from the wagon. Skye started her walk towards the white Mercantile building. When she opened the door, a bell rang as she entered.

"Good morning, malady!"

"Good morning, sir."

"What can I help you with this fine day?"

"I'd like 4 eggs, some of that dried sausage, and this small basket, please," Skye said with a smile.

"You must be new in town."

"We are."

"I figured as much. Not many people come in looking for baskets or eggs around here."

"Well, we are just passing through."

"I understand. If you need a place to stay, there's an inn down a ways from here."

"Thank you for your kindness, but we are just passing through to meet with some kin."

"Not a problem. Just thought I'd mention it because there's a new cook named Zhang there. Best food I have ever tasted, I tell you!"

"Zhang?"

"That's right."

"Well, we just may have to stop by after all," Skye said as she took her purchases and left the mercantile. She wanted to get back to Raine quickly and tell him about Zhang.

Skye reached the wagon in record time, only to see that Raine had already caught up with Zhang.

"Hey, sweetness. Look who I ran into!"

"I was just coming to tell you that Zhang was in town."

"Come to the inn. We have much to discuss. A lot has happened since I last saw you in Colorado."

Raine and Skye got into the wagon with Zhang and headed for the inn. Zhang got them a room and told them to meet him downstairs.

Skye and Raine went to their room to settle in and wash up before they went downstairs for supper.

The room was cozy and simple. There was only a three-drawer dresser in dark cherry wood and a modest-sized bed in the brightly lit room.

"It's a nice room. I'm glad we can stay here for the evening. Sleeping on rocks isn't the most comfortable, and I welcome a soft bed for my tired bones." Skye pulled the white lace curtain from the window to look out.

Raine pulled Skye close to his waist.

"I know, but I was hoping that your tired bones didn't want to sleep too much this evening." He said as he drew his lips towards hers for a soft, short kiss.

"I may need to be persuaded a little more." Skye tousled his hair with her fingers.

"I think I can oblige a little more persuasion for you, but later." His lips brushed her forehead for a brief kiss. "Right now, we need to get downstairs and meet with Zhang."

* * *

Raine and Skye sat in the deserted dining area just as Zhang came out with two dinner plates.

"There are times that your psychic powers scare

me. We've barely sat down. How could you know we were here already?"

"Sorry. Sometimes I forget that people are not used to my psychic forwardness. I just assume they know this side of me."

"I will be back shortly with my own plate."

"Oh? I thought we would have to wait to talk to you after you serve everyone supper." Skye asked.

"You two are the only customers I have for the evening and the only two people staying at the inn."

"I see. How convenient. Again, there are times when you scare me, old man."

"Who are you calling old, Raine?" Zhang said with a chuckle. "All kidding aside, I must tell you of my vision. It came to me two nights after you left me in Colorado. I decided to follow you here because it is not a good vision. Alec and Armand will be coming after you here. Their plan to destroy your lineage failed."

"Here? But we are not ready. I thought Skye was supposed to get a vision from Durga before the confrontation. It's just too soon."

"You should know by now, after seeing one major prophecy die and the other wanting to kill you, that the gods do not always keep their promises, Raine."

"Perhaps I was just hoping, Skye."

"For a miracle? Eh? I don't think that will happen unless the goddess Durga manifests into the gods again." Zhang said as he took a large bite of his stew. "In my vision walk, I saw Shiva, and he said that the brothers cannot be taken on together. The only way to stop them is to divide them."

"That makes very little sense, Zhang. Are the gods just playing with us again? Why do they have to speak so cryptically?" Skye said in disgust.

"Shiva said that should make the most sense to you. Perhaps your understanding will come when you see Durga?"

Skye lowered her head. She knew Durga did not want them to know of her vision, but it was becoming too difficult to keep up the lie.

"I have already seen Durga, and she did not mention such a thing."

"Skye? Why didn't you tell me?"

"The vision was just too much. I couldn't tell you, Raine."

"But she had to show you something that could help us," Zhang said.

"All she showed me was the two of us taking a blood oath and then dying by Alec's hand. How could that possibly help us defeat the brothers?"

"You are right. That doesn't make sense unless the gods want the witches and vampires feuding for millennia." Raine said.

"Zhang, is there a way for us to invoke her?" Skye asked. "I'm sure she doesn't mean to have the entire prophecy die with all of us."

"We most certainly can try, but not here. We will set out for the mountains after supper. They are not that far, and we can be back here for a good night's rest."

* * *

The three set out towards the mountains after Zhang cleaned up and gathered a collection of thyme, basil, lemongrass, and parsley for the smudging they would do before the spirit walk.

Skye tried to smooth out some wrinkles on her dress to keep her mind off the reoccurring images in her head. She hoped that Zhang could help her understand why Durga only showed her their death.

They entered the first cave and set up a small camp. Zhang prepared the fire and the herb bundle and had Skye stand. Raine watched as Zhang smudged her head, followed by her torso and legs.

Skye could already see Durga manifesting before them in the fire.

"Brightest Blessings, my daughter and sons!"

"Well, this is different," Raine said as he stood up to face the fire and Durga. "How come we can hear you now?"

"I have taken on the form of Shiva, so I can speak to you all."

"Why did you only show me our deaths? Aren't we supposed to fulfill the prophecy?" Skye interjected.

"You will be. But it will not be during this lifetime. That is why I wanted you to use the water to your advantage. You need to release your fears from this life before you can propel to the next."

"The next? I don't want a next! I want this one now with Raine!" Skye protested.

"Child, you are both forever tied to each other. Your bond started in 300 BC and is stronger than any mortal or immortal could conceive."

"How will we find each other? Doesn't free will play a part in all of this?" Raine asked.

"It does play a part, but that is minimal where you are concerned. I will give you some new gifts in your next life so that you may defeat Alec. Raine, you will be bestowed the power of tracking Skye and Alec, and Skye, you will continue to have your psychic abilities. But they will not be as strong as they are now. With every gift I bestow, a balance has to occur. Your new gift is the power to cast any spell with the help of the goddesses you choose to invoke."

"What about Armand?" Zhang asked.

"He will not be your concern. Fate will separate the twins so that balance is restored."

"And just how exactly will all this happen?" Skye asked.

"You and Raine will have to perform the blood oath when the time comes. It is the only way Raine can track you in the 21st century."

Skye swallowed hard. They were barely in the

14th century. Seven centuries seemed too long to be away from her love.

"Time knows no bounds, Skye. Trust in the journey that the gods have brought to you. Especially since you leave this time and go directly to the 21st century." Durga said as her image disappeared in the ambers of the fire.

Another mist started to form just inside the cave. Skye thought it was Durga again. She began to walk over to the fog when the color changed from silver to green.

"Skye! That's not Durga! Hurry!" Raine said to her as he grabbed her hand.

He led her towards a densely wooded area where they found a large rock to hide behind. Streams of light shot over the rock, formed into energy balls, and burned the earth as they hit the ground.

Raine pulled Skye close to his waist and caressed her cheek.

"We have to do this. There is no other way. You know they are too powerful for us here; perhaps the gods will see that the 21st century will be kinder to us. I love you, sweetness."

Raine took out of his pocket a small knife. An onyx stone was set into a white pearl-colored handle. He slid the knife across the palm of his hand, and crimson red droplets formed within moments of him touching the blade.

He drew her closer to him and placed lips gently

but briefly on Skye's. She wished the tenderness of the kiss were not as brief as it was. Far too many of their last kisses had been short, thanks to Alec.

"You are my forever, sweetness," Raine whispered.

Skye nodded and took in her last breath of him. "I love you with all of my soul." She felt a prick on her hand as Raine slashed her palm with the knife.

Skye pulled the dragonfly necklace Raine fashioned for her off her neck and intertwined it with the blood flowing from her palm.

Raine clasped her hand and started to recite an all too familiar oath. They chose the one for their wedding, which paid homage to Skye's paternal grandmother. She repeated it with him.

"You are blood of my blood and bone of my bone. I give you my body that we two are one. I give you my spirit till life as we know it is done."

They were no sooner finished when Alec destroyed the rock they were hiding behind. Zhang stepped in front of Alec.

"Alec! You do not wish to do this, boy."

Alec pushed Zhang aside.

"Stay out of this, Zhang. My problems are not with you, and you need to remain the neutral sorcerer you are!" Alec spat.

The force of Alec's blow to Zhang sent him toward a large oak tree where his head met the trunk.

"Zhang!" Skye shrilled to his motionless body.

Skye could feel the steady flow of crimson coming down their clasped wrists. She saw some droplets penetrate the earth before she felt the first blow from Alec's fist.

She fell to her knees. Raine rushed between the two of them and hit Alec in the gut. Alec only smiled as he picked up Raine by his throat.

Raine released his grip from Skye and clutched his throat, trying desperately to break Alec's hold on him.

Skye, disorientated from her blow, tried to grasp for Alec's leg to pull him down. She found his leg but had no strength to push his knee in. She looked up to see Raine take his last human breath and let out a curdling cry.

Alec dropped Raine's limp body in front of Skye, and she crawled over to him. She knew she had only seconds to mourn him and tried to make the best of it. She reached for his lips and kissed them swiftly while closing his eyes.

"You and he are the reason I lost Obsidian! Watching him die is your punishment. And make no mistake. He will one day see you die by my hand as well. This is not over." Alec said to her as he reached for her neck with both hands and swiftly snapped it.

EIGHT

MERIDEN, CT, USA MAY 8, 2014

The images faded as quickly as they came when Skye opened her eyes. She turned over in bed, startled by her alarm, and tried to shut it off.

She cupped her face as she looked out at her bedroom window. It was morning again, and these dreams would not stop. This one was even more bizarre than the last few and felt strangely familiar.

The whole thing kept plaguing her. She had to know the truth from Raine and today. Skye reached for her evening purse and pulled up the cell phone number he had given her the night before.

She texted.

> Meet me for coffee at Java Max at 10 AM sharp

And then she hit send before her nerves got the best of her.

Within seconds, a response appeared on her cell screen.

Okay

Skye shook off her uncertainty about being with him the night before with a flip of her hair. She had never trusted a man, let alone pursue one on her own by boldly asking for his number. It was not something she was ever raised to do. Skye showered, put on a comfortable, light pink sweater and black leggings, and headed for the coffee shop.

The shop was bustling in the late morning hours. A bell on the door announced a man dressed rather peculiarly for New England's Christmas weather. As his cowboy boots clicked on the wet tile floor, the crowd seemed to quiet their roar.

Skye had never seen him before, although a chill of familiarity stung her neck as she watched him order.

His dark eyes were too piercing for her comfort as he glanced her way. The man then walked out with his shot of espresso.

Raine walked in just as the man was leaving. Their eyes met for an instant, and Skye could see the distaste Raine had for the man in his eyes.

His gaze then softened once they met hers. He then quickly sat in the empty chair of the two-top that Skye was sitting in.

"You now know, don't you?"

"I'm not sure what you mean?" Skye said as she nervously played with her napkin.

"You've had dreams. Haven't you? Dreams about us?"

"Yes. How did you know?"

"Because I have been too. I know your dreams because you have projected them onto me for the past several nights. Skye, this isn't a coincidence that we met at Backtracks. We are kindred spirits. I know you know that."

"I think I do, but?" Her voice trailed.

"Let me ask you something. Last night you dreamed about a 14th-century lifetime where we performed a blood oath, a spell we performed so that it keeps us together in each lifetime."

"Yes," Skye said in a whisper. She was astonished that Raine could explain the dream so vividly.

Skye's soul stirred. She was starting to remember everything. Alec, the stranger in cowboy boots, was still after them, and they needed to vanquish that King of the Vlads.

"What do we need to do?"

"Train."

"Okay. When do we start?"

"After this cup of coffee at my place, sweetness."

he End For Now...
Read Forever Immortal for the outcome.

BEFORE YOU GO...

Did you enjoy Forever Tied? If so, you can sign up for my newsletter where I offer more fun and freebies!
https://www.authoramandakimberley.com/newsletter-signup

IF YOU LIKE FOREVER TIED YOU MIGHT LIKE...

MANIFESTATIONS

USA TODAY BEST SELLING AUTHOR

AMANDA KIMBERLEY

MANIFESTATIONS
CHAPTER ONE

The house was perfect. It had everything on her wish list, large updated kitchen and great room for entertaining. A decent sized yard for the dog she had always wanted. And it even overlooked Masterbon pond, a bonus since she loved water.

The master bath's new fixtures and glass tiles glistened in the sunlight. The feature of the room, however, was the claw-footed tub that anchored the large picture window, a divine feature for any woman. But the best feature of all had to be the huge walk-in closet, which equaled the size of her entire studio apartment.

Heather Young's belly grew tight with fear to ask the realtor the listing price of this gem. It became painfully doubtful that this spacious beauty could be in her price range. Deep within her gut, she found she didn't care. Heather wanted the house and started to possess a need to do everything in her power to get it no matter what the cost.

She started a hunt for things wrong with the place in hopes of striking up a good deal, but her attempts proved feeble since the water pressure looked good and so did the pipes, roof, foundation, and furnace.

Heather Young loved a good buy. She looked for them everywhere in her life. Bargain hunting became a thrill even though she seldom shopped for herself. When she did, she had a set price in mind before she ventured out the door. Her budget always dangled over her like a hangover. She rarely swayed from it.

A must-have item didn't exist in her vocabulary, especially at full price. Clearance became a way of life for her, in fact, she considered those racks family and not just a mere friend. Getting things at a decent price proved to be a matter of principle to her, especially since she understood that clothing had a 70 percent markup, a little tidbit of information she had learned many years ago while working retail management.

The other side to this principal is business economics. Simply put, if she started buying that must-have item at a ridiculously high price just because she wanted it, the item would stay at a ridiculously high price simply because someone bought it for that amount. This, she judged to be completely unfair to others since the average American found it nearly impossible to purchase anything these days.

It became more of a sense of duty to Heather to hold out. If she showed some restraint, prices would be reasonable for her and other consumers. Heather never called herself cheap, but she believed Ben Franklin would approve her frugality.

"It's going for $180,000." The realtor said.

Heather's eyes widened with each word forming from the Realtor's lips. She found it hard to fathom what she heard and almost asked the realtor to repeat herself, but as Heather opened her mouth, a twinge swelled in her belly and her throat went dry.

That listing price was a huge bargain in the state of Connecticut, Plymouth especially. She didn't want to even gander as to why a house like this priced for so low on the market but assumed it had to have something to do with the housing bubble bursting. This a great deal and one she'd easily afford, so she put in a bid and crossed her fingers and toes.

The next morning came and no phone call from the realtor graced Heather's cell. She bit her lip slightly while glancing at the sparse notifications she did receive on her phone and replaying thoughts of yesterday.

A bid of $170,000, $10,000 lower than the asking price, may not have been wise but at the time her paranoia of looking too desperate for the house had outweighed her hindsight on the deal. Heather haggling for a better price did not prove to be a foreign concept to her, especially if she had wiggle room.

She reached for her coffee and perused the morning paper. Heather let out a sigh, figuring she should get a head start on a new house search since this one may not pan out. Her heart started to sink as she turned to the classifieds. She really hoped to get that place, but it looked like she'd be facing another disappointment.

Disappointments became pretty commonplace in Heather's life. Her father was the poster child of disappointment since birth. He may have been physically around for her, but he lacked major skills to provide her with emotional support. Sure, he'd make a ton of jokes to lift her sad spirits if she skinned her knee or had a bad break up while in high school. But he became the absent father for recitals and his humor grew unbearable when lending sound advice for tough financial decisions.

She found it hard to lay all the blame squarely on him though. His mother, Heather's estranged Grandmother, was like him. The whole family tree possessed the same emotionally closed off trait. None of them seemed to like to talk.

Heather peered over at her kitchen clock to check the time. It read 7 AM, and she needed to start heading out for work. She hated leaving an hour and a half early to beat the morning rush hour and longed for the tiring commute from Norwalk to Hartford to come to an end. Plymouth was only a 20-minute drive, a bat of the eyelash. Her heart sank again as she gulped down the last swig of her coffee.

Heather's job was not an easy one. The head of human resources for a large insurance company in Hartford is not a job for the thin-skinned. Her morning greetings became a constant line of employees begging for her time to discuss personal days or vacation matters.

She didn't mind this so much when she first started. The newness and excitement to land a great paying job fresh out of college made her wide-eyed outlook on life easier to bear. But the relentlessly long workdays started to creep up on her. She never seemed to finish what she wanted to accomplish at day's start and would find herself being one of the last employees to leave at 8 PM. The stress of the added commute did not help matters because she wouldn't get home until 10.

Heather sighed as she turned the key of her Sorento.

God, I hope I don't have to trek so far for much longer.

Connecticut was a nice place to live because it had all four seasons but the people on the roadways seemed to be stuck in the cold. They weren't like

New Yorkers who'd at least signal you with their finger before they decided to cut you off. No Connecticut drivers were a special kind of breed. They viewed turn signals as a sign of weakness, not a sign of common courtesy.

Driving stressed Heather out so much that she had almost considered taking up smoking again. She had quit five years ago because she developed asthma, but she truly wanted to throw caution to the wind every time she got into the car and drove the highways of Connecticut. Sure smoking may be bad for her. It may prove to kill her, one day, but the jackasses on the road may do a number on her too. A slow agonizing death by choice seemed more enticing than one done by the hands of a brainless, road-raged idiot.

The hardest fact to wrap her head around became the lack of down time once she reached the parking garage for The Hartford. Her colleagues always seemed to bombard her with a ton of questions that really had very little to do with her job title. Yes, her office door had human resources on the front, and that meant she had an idea of exactly how many days an employee had as paid personal time off, along with a few other benefit perks that baffled the common employee, but she had nothing to do with payroll.

HR managers that ran payroll proved to be a special kind of breed. They had to be tough as nails on the job because no one seemed to value their time. Employees always seemed to think that an HR person had all the time in the world to answer questions that very easily can be looked up on the employee website. These employees never seemed to grasp the fact that it took time to pay people.

An HR person did not eat bonbons all day as these employees seemed to assume. They actually had work to perform and if said HR person grew constantly interrupted throughout the day, it may not bode well in the employee's paycheck. Mistakes happened, and oh how Heather wished she had the authority to make one, or even twenty of those mistakes happen on a weekly basis.

She hated paying people for this reason and thankful that she didn't have any part of it after her college internship ended. Heather liked her HR Management Claims position because it allowed her the freedom to award employee performance creatively. Recruitment proved to be another fun part of the job because she liked networking. She had been often told that she had the gift of gab.

Today's agenda would be a little different. She'd be in meetings with higher management all day. Her only break would be lunch where she needed to catch up on calls among other things. Judy, her assistant, came in with a pile of phone messages seconds after Heather put her lunch on her desk.

Heather adored Judy as the perfect assistant,

paying attention to every detail. She filtered all calls by order of importance. Any from the boss came first, followed by inquiries. Anything of a personal nature came before work, which became a perk Heather grew to love about Judy. Heather noticed that the realtor had left a message in the personal pile of messages and held her breath as she made the return call.

"I just wanted to call you to tell you that you are a home owner! Congratulations! The bid went through!"

Heather's mind started spinning with color schemes and interior decor as she hung on every word from the realtor. She smiled and bounced a little in her chair when the realtor told her to prepare for a closing in one week. She thought it odd that the buyers bit so quickly, but the realtor assured her that there was nothing strange about it. The house had been on the market for quite some time due to the housing slump and the buyers grew eager to get the house off their hands.

The closing date came and passed almost as quickly as the keys did in Heather's hand. She held them as tight and as endearing as a child would with a stuffed animal. The house, just over the Bristol border on 66 Todd Hollow Road in Plymouth, CT finally became her unbelievable miracle.

She rushed to her now newly owned home and slowly unlocked the door. She wanted to savor this moment in her memory. Her legs started to tingle and twinge as she reached over the threshold. Her ankles grew heavy and became increasingly harder to move. She grabbed her right thigh and as she peered at her legs, she noticed a whirl of whitish mist swirl around her torso. She perceived this odd because she had a good day and no noticeable pain from her Fibromyalgia, nor did she experience any problems stemming from her debilitating migraines. So she decided to chalk it all up to living in the moment.

Heather started putting her bed together first. She really wanted to tackle the kitchen, but the setting sun as a backdrop in her large picture window reminded her of the lateness of the day. A good night sleep before work on Friday morning outweighed her need for an orderly kitchen. She planned for the weekend off so she'd have time to put the bulk of the boxes from the move away.

Heather liked to have everything in order. She didn't have major OCD tendencies by any means like her mother did, but she did like order none the less and that always seemed most appropriate in the kitchen.

Moving became a common occurrence for her in her twenties. She needed a break from her domi-neering mother and absent father and crashing at her friends' places, or even a boyfriend's proved second nature for her. It's not that she perceived herself possessing abandonment issues like her father had by leaving the minute someone got too close to her, on the contrary, she saw it as a growing period in her life.

Heather had a taste of being on her own in high school. Her chorus class took a trip to Canada for a whole week of blissful freedom where she ate where she wanted to. Slept when she wanted to and hung out with who she wanted to. She didn't even give her family more than a thought until they had started the trek home. Sure her mind gravitated towards them while in the tourist gift shops, but other than that, she did not make any phone calls claiming homesickness.

Living alone was great except for the quietness of the night. Heather found it hard to get used to that. Her house growing up always had some kind of noise like a stereo, television set, or rumble of the occasional motorcycle from the Polish Club nearby. The stillness of the night used to drive her crazy, which is why she liked to always move.

As Heather got into bed, a cool breeze brushed her arm. She found that a bit odd for a 90 degree May night, but dismissed it. Her air conditioner blasted on high from a window in another part of the room so she had no need to ponder such silly notions of a chill in the air and started to drift off to sleep.

"Go into the attic and you will find me there."

The man said as he appeared towards Heather dressed in a Confederate soldier uniform. "There are some papers I must show you in the suitcase." The man continued.

He was a slender gentleman with blond hair and long sideburns. Heather couldn't tell for sure, but he looked well defined under that uniform and the heat in his azure blue eyes blazed like they would melt the Arctic.

"I will wait for you at daybreak." He said while stroking her cheek. His touch sent a chill down her spine that felt all too familiar. His gazed met hers and the heat in his eyes surged through to her core.

Not this time. I will not be duped again by a gorgeous face.

The new move was not only to relocate closer to her work but to put some distance between her and Brady as well. That breakup proved hard and a rebound would make things extremely complicated, yet, Heather found it difficult to understand why a dream held this much attention to her introspection of men.

The buzzer from the alarm sounded as Heather began to stretch under the covers. She shook her head to try to get the cobwebs out while remembering her dream. Heather grew puzzled as to why she'd dream of a soldier.

The TV blared as she walked by it on her way to the shower. She remembered falling asleep while

Ghost Adventurers aired and vaguely recalled one of them putting on a uniform to provoke evidence from spirits of the Civil war.

No more night time TV for me.

Still, as the water rained down on her face, she couldn't help but wonder about the dream. The bit about the attic and a suitcase left her curious. It wouldn't hurt to check it out. After all, she had a few extra minutes before work now that she didn't have to commute for an hour and a half.

Feeling a bit silly as she slipped into her robe and slippers, she headed up the staircase leading to the attic. The house's old Victorian layout boasted four floors. Heather didn't need so much space for herself but had hoped to one day renovate the house's first floor into a homeopathic store. A silly pipe dream she'd had for many years, but now with the space, seemed more like a reality.

The attic door was locked during her showing because the realtor didn't have the right set of keys that day. Heather considered it odd that the owner would have locked the door during a showing, but she figured there must have been some valuables they staged in there for the move.

A cold winter-like breeze stung Heather's bare legs as she opened the door.

Guess I'll have to rezone the heat in this place along with adding some insulation. Heather thought while trying to hug herself warm.

Some sunlight pierced through a tiny hole in the thick mauve pink drapes carelessly left by the prior owner, highlighting a tattered, mahogany colored suitcase. She couldn't be certain, because her eyes always played tricks on her in the early morning hours, but it almost looked like it opened by itself.

A piece of paper peeked through the crack in the case and Heather pulled it out. It appeared to be a love letter from a soldier to his fiancée. The letter read like an all-too familiar 16th-century poem from Shakespeare.

My Dearest Gwen,

I love thee more than life itself. The days and nights without you have been far too long for me to bear. I pray that this war ends soon so I can be with you and we can start our lives together.

A rush of heat came to Heather's cheeks. She felt foolish reading someone else's love letter, but she found it hard to resist.

I miss the touch of your hand on my cheek, the smell of your hair, the fullness of your lips, and the crux neck. I also miss the cleavage between your bosoms. My body aches for your closeness each day and night that we are apart.

Heather's eyes fixated to the paper, hovering over every word, hanging on whole paragraphs like she once did on each rung of a monkey bar as a child. She craved for more in each word and sentence as if reading her favorite romance author.

Her heart beat fast and her breath, shorten as she read on.

I long for the day we can celebrate our love for each other, consummating what our minds have known for years, a blissful, sweet, enduring love that knows no bounds. Hold fast to these words, my sweetness for I shall come home to you soon.

A cool tingle came down Heather's cheek. Feeling flustered, she folded the letter up and placed it back in the suitcase for safe keeping. As she descended the stairs a cool breeze wrapped around her shoulders. Heather crossed her arms to ward off the coolness.

*

It grew difficult to keep any focus at work. Those heartfelt words from the love letters burned into Heather's soul. She had never known a love to be so deep, yet her heart yearned to come across one. A soul mate in this day and age proved hard to find and if you came across that kind of love in your life-time, you considered yourself extremely lucky.

With a letter like that, Heather wondered what other kinds of treasures lay hidden in the attic. The suspense killed her, but she had one more hour before she officially ended her day.

The hour drew on for days but it finally ended and Heather again found herself rummaging through an attic that seemed almost untouched by the prior tenants. It was almost as if they had abandoned the room altogether.

Another cold breeze came across Heather's cheeks and this time, she saw a mist form from it. The mist materialized into a hand, which made Heather kilter off balance. She assumed a migraine was taking over her clear-headed thoughts, yet this seemed different.

A ripple of arousal came over her as the materialized hand cup her breast. Heather lay still in amazement. A man hadn't touched her in so long that she wondered if those parts even worked. Her mind grew erratic with questions.

Why am I feeling this way now? I'm awake! I usually don't have sexually connotative dreams unless it's at night.

"Stop your rationalization, sweetness."

Heather couldn't believe her ears, nor her eyes. A man came out of nothing and appeared right before her. He was tall and proportioned with light hair and blue eyes and everything Heather could dream of in a man, right down to a chiseled chin. Her heart skipped a beat upon seeing this man before her, but her mind started the double take.

She had not been with a man in ages and her mind must have gotten the best of her. Her fantasies had to be running into overdrive and that must be the reason for this Casanova to materialize before her in a daydream like state.

"I'm not a figment of your imagination, Heather. I'm just as real as you are."

Are you as real as I am? What the hell is going on? Good Lord, I need a shrink.

Within an instant, the man vanished as quickly as he materialized. Heather shook her head and decided to go about her day as if nothing had happened.

*

A few weeks had gone by and Heather grew giddy planning her first dinner party at her new home. Holidays had always been big in her family so she didn't want to take on the stress of a huge gathering during the approaching holiday season and opted for a summer gathering instead. She always liked celebrating during the warmest months of the year because she could be herself.

Cookouts may have seemed informal to most people, but Heather found them liberating. It was the only time she was free from the stressful constrictions of family gatherings. Friends had always been easy to entertain, and for some reason, they tended to drink far less than her family members did, another bonus for someone who enjoyed being able to be herself.

This gathering would be more special than most though because Derik would be right by her side. Derik was the breath of fresh air she had been looking for. He listened to her, had always been attentive to her feelings, and a tall, dark, and handsome man to boot. She couldn't ask for anything more in a man and she was happy they'd be entertaining their friends together as a couple tonight.

Their whirlwind affair may have caught Heather a bit off guard, but their wedding date was far enough off in advance where she had some time if she needed to think about their quick bond. The thing with Derik was that she felt she didn't need to worry. He grew more perfect with each day.

Everything seemed to be going well in her life except for the house. Heather hoped she wouldn't have to contend with any problems tonight with her darling little money pit. She should have trusted her gut when she had found out how cheap the house listed for and wished she had known then what she knew now.

The infestation of flies had been the first thing to go wrong, then the faucets built up enough pressure where they were practically turning on by themselves. The kitchen cabinet doors never seemed to stay closed and the noises in the basement stirred a fear in Heather that made her believe the furnace might be going.

First-time home ownership was terrifying to

Heather, and she grew relieved with the fact that she now had Derik to lean on. He seemed to have an answer for all of her problems with the house and that comforted Heather since she had no one else to rely on when it came to home repairs.

The only thing that bothered Heather about her relationship with Derik was the fact that he practiced Witchcraft. Heather understood that Derik couldn't turn anyone into a toad or fly on a broom, but he did have a cauldron that he used on occasion to whip up potions with.

She was an old school devote Catholic who had been raised in believing that that sort of stuff is devil worshiping. She hated going against her own core values. It almost killed her inside. But nothing Derik did proved to be evil. In fact, he seemed more Christian than some of the avid church goers in her parish. She also wasn't getting any younger and on her 40th birthday, she came to the conclusion that she had been too picky as far as men were concerned.

Derik wasn't someone she settled for by any stretch of the means, he truly was a wonderful and gentle man. She was just uncomfortable with the fact that he may cast a curse upon her if he didn't like the way she starched his shirts.

*

A meaty, flavorful lasagna came along with nightfall. Heather set out carefully constructed place settings for each of her dinner guests as the main course cooled. An ear piercing clank came from the basement as she placed the last wine goblet on the dining table. She let out a sigh and muttered a Hail Mary as she shuffled down the stairs to see what was wrong.

The furnace was rather old and still boasted a window and flapper. Heather knew she'd have to replace it at some point but the building inspector, who had passed the house with flying colors, assured her that she wouldn't have to replace the contraption for another few years.

Heather beamed a flashlight into one of the suspected culprits, a duct directly underneath the dining room that notoriously collects dust faster than all the rest of the rooms. She was surprised to find nothing but metal reflecting back at her. Heather sighed again as she climbed the stairs. Another thing to add to the list of things to do for the house. She thought.

Upon ascending into the kitchen, she came to the realization that her mother was right about one thing a house is a child that never grows up. She desperately hoped that her house could shut up in a time out long enough for her to enjoy herself at the gathering, but deep down she knew she might be asking for too much.

A cold breeze came over her as she started to open the Moscato. She shut the window in the kitchen and clasped her upper arms in a shiver. Heather always loved a brisk breeze at night, but the coolness was getting to her this summer. She garnished the final parsley piece on the lasagna when Derik walked in.

"This is going to be so much fun! I just love Beltane!" Derik said while putting a bundle of kindling wood and package of rice cakes down on the kitchen counter. "These are for my clan. No need for you to fret over them. We are going to do a working tonight after the non-practitioners leave."

"Okay?" Heather said in her unusually inquisitive tone. She still had a hard time grasping the whole witch thing. In her ignorant attempts to try to understand him, she called him a warlock. Heather had no idea that such a term was actually an insult to any male practitioner since the term originally meant traitor. It took her quite some time to stop calling him that.

"We are going to do a house blessing tonight— among other things."

"I see. Well, hope everything turns out okay." Heather managed to muster before the doorbell signified their first guests of the evening.

*

Heather wasn't sure if the absence of noise from her basement was due to the plethora of wine she consumed this evening to forget about her money pit, or if those noises just had a mind of their own. Derik was nice enough to always scout out every creak and clank the house made, but she was really starting to wonder if she was becoming certifiable.

"I don't want to wig you out or anything, Heather, but there's a lot of stuff going on around here that isn't just about the house settling. You've got an uninvited guest living with you in this place and that's why we are going to do the blessing." Derik said quietly and flatly during one of their trips to the kitchen.

"I'm sorry, what?" Heather said in disbelief. Here she was thinking about her own madness and now she's being faced with Derik's mentally deranged visions of ghosts inhabiting her money pit. "Are you talking about me having ghosts in my house again?"

"Yes, yes I am. And they are more like malevolent spirits, but ghosts none the less."

"I see." Heather said while taking another sip of wine. "Okay." She wasn't sure what else she should add to the conversation. It was weird enough without her extra drivel.

"I will need you to hold the candle in tonight's working, Heather, but don't worry we will do the rest."

Heather started to feel the sensation of bile

coming up from stomach and trailing towards her mouth. She wanted no part in this working. These rituals frightened her to no end, but he would be her husband one day and it really wouldn't bode well for them if she decided to cop out now. She nodded in acceptance to the task.

COMING SOON...

FOREVER *loved*

USA TODAY BEST SELLING AUTHOR

AMANDA KIMBERLEY

SNEAK PEAK OF FOREVER LOVED

Lilith opened her eyes and sucked in her first breath as she took in all the purple blooms hanging from a vine in front of her. Warmth caressed her bare, pale skin, but she wasn't sure where the heat was coming from just yet.

"She is beautiful. More than I could have ever dreamed, Jade Emperor Yudi!"

"I call her Lilith, Adam. And she is born from the same dust as you. She is your equal in every way. You will live together here in my garden as long as you wish to."

Lilith shook her head. The words she was hearing seemed fuzzy. It was as if she heard the voices while inside a cave.

"I promise to love her with all my soul as you have asked me to, Yudi."

Warm and solid arms were now cradling her

waist and hoisting her upright. Still weak from awakening, Lilith fell into a chiseled torso that radiated heat so strong it was as if she was standing next to light itself. She screwed her eyes shut in fear of the light blinding her.

A hard object hit her inner thigh. She tried to shift her weight to alleviate the painful pinch penetrating her womanhood. But the more that she struggled against the tweak, the more she realized there wasn't much pain at all. Desire seemed to replace the pain she initially experienced, and she found her body responding to the wealth of pleasure growing deep within her belly.

"I will leave you both to grow my garden with your children." Said the voice Lilith now knew belonged to Yudi.

The strong arms that had lifted her to her feet now guided her down to a soft bed of leaves and vines.

"You are beautiful, Lilith, and you are all mine. I love you."

"I love you, too."

She found herself reiterating the words. And strangely, she somehow knew what they meant without being told. She loved this man. A man Yudi called Adam. A sharp pain hit her belly again as something hard slipped between her thighs once more. It was comparable to a small hurt, something Lilith could deal with. However, she was becoming more and more aware of her surroundings as she awoke from the sleep that was thick enough to refrain her from any clear thinking. Her body soon stiffened as Adam's lips grazed her cheek.

"I'm sorry! Am I doing something to hurt you? I don't mean to! Please tell me what it is you desire, and I will be forthright in obliging such."

Lilith opened her eyes, and a person, whom she knew to be a man without question, was staring back at her. He had gorgeous green eyes. They were as verdant as the vines surrounding them.

YOU MAY ALSO LIKE...

EQUIPOISE SOLAR SYSTEM SERIES
Laying Claim to the Lion
USA TODAY BEST SELLING AUTHOR
AMANDA KIMBERLEY

LAYING CLAIM TO THE LION

"This isn't an option, Verena. If you don't want to marry, you have no choice but to find a suitable male to conceive an heir. Jaxson saw to it that the Valet de Chambre isn't in our favor. And after the Battle of Quell, we appear weak."

Tilda stroked Verena's chestnut hair to braid it. She formed four strands to make a sizeable French braid with Verena's dark locks.

"So what do you expect me to do, Tilda? It's not like our planet has any males on it! And with Jaxson taking over almost all the Equipoise solar system, I won't find anyone willing to defy him."

Verena sighed as she turned to meet Tilda's gaze.

"You certainly can't give into Jaxson. He may want you as his queen, but you know mating with him will be a certain sentence to slavery. Not to mention what it will mean for the rest of our pride.

We've always had an option to seek a mate from any planet of our choosing. But if Jaxson gets his way, none of them are safe. We will be forced to only mate with the people of Emir." Said Tilda.

"I would never think of giving in to him. That panther is simply barbaric! But finding a mate who isn't under Jaxson's tyranny will be hard."

"Earth would be your best option. That solar system is several galaxies away and has never heard of Jaxson. But you must be careful there. Many of the humans on Earth can not shift, and what's worse is that most of them do not believe in shifters. The people are primitive, but if you stick to your feminity, you will find a mate in enough time."

Verena frowned and gripped the guild-colored arm of her thrown. She massaged the lion-carved paw that protruded and curled around the bottom of the arm, hoping the gesture would allow her the privilege of perspective.

"Verena, there are some shifters on that planet, and your abilities will allow you to sense they are. However, they are not as advanced as us. Many of the men are as barbaric as Jaxson. Very possessive, very domineering. But some are suitable mates for an heir."

Tilda shrugged her shoulders and peered out the large glass window that overlooked the lush kingdom. Her eyes fixed on the rainforest that was a little past the main village. A rainbow was forming, and

Tilda smiled. That seemed like a good omen, but she also always loved to meditate on them. And with Effeminate's future hanging in the balance, she could use all the meditating she could find.

"That wasn't what was really bothering me. Shifter or not, it really doesn't matter. I just need the man's seed. I'm not going there to find a mate. The Valet de Chambre's decree merely states that we need an heir. Therefore, I don't need to bring home a mate."

Tilda blinked a few times and then gazed into Verena's eyes.

"What do you mean, you aren't going there to find a mate? We need a king. A king will protect us from Jaxson's tyranny."

Verena stood up and narrowed her eyes as she gazed at Tilda and walked past her towards the window. She placed her hands on the sill and looked out at the vast green jungle, farmlands, and stone buildings that made up the planet she had loved and cared for since birth. Verena pointed out toward the stone-engineered buildings that looked like the pyramids of Earth they once helped the Egyptians build.

"Look at all of them. These women are brilliant and strong. They do not need any male to help protect them, nor do they need a male to construct a building for them. We women of Effeminate built a foundation of powerful warriors in our own right, and I will not let one battle determine our downfall."

"Verena, it may have only been one battle, but it was one that killed your parents and extended this war into several hundred cycles. There's also no end in sight. As your general, I think it's wise for us to explore other options to end it. Especially now that the panther shifters have taken over all but two planets in our solar system. It's just us and the planet Tatsu who are not under Jaxson's thumb."

"Jaxson will never overthrow the dragon shifters. He's not powerful enough to defeat Dragon Jilocasin of Tatsu."

"True, but it is only a matter of time where even the Tatsus will be against us. It's not like those overgrown reptiles have been friendly with any warm-blooded cat ever before. None of the treaties apply to them because of how cold-blooded they are. They don't practice diplomacy. All they seem to do is produce law as part of the council without seeing first-hand how that law will affect any planet. No, the only way to fight off Jaxson is if we find some alphas to help us defeat him. Planet Emir won't have a chance against the shifter species of Earth. I just know it. And besides, your own mother believed in the value of having a male mate from the planet Earth. Having a partner gives you perspective when leading your great people."

Tilda placed her hand on Verena's shoulder. Verena brushed it off.

"Yes, and look at what that value got her! She's dead, Tilda, and so is my father! I can do nothing about that except fight Jaxson without showing weakness. And I believe my father was my mother's downfall. Her love for him was why she fell in battle." Verena crossed her arms and shook her head before continuing, "Her head was too clouded with love. That's why she didn't see that panther coming for her. She was so fixated on the one killing my father. No! I will not allow our sisters to be clouded with love, fear, or apprehension. They don't need to be tied down to a man. They need to focus on this war. We will win the Ebb War and in honor of my mother!" Verena clenched fists. "Now, please prepare my ship for my solo trip to Earth."

"You don't plan on having an escort?"

"What do I need protection from, Tilda? You said it yourself. These shifters are primitive compared to us. I shouldn't need any help with them or finding a suitable seed."

"Yes, my Queen," Tilda bowed before continuing. "How long do you plan on staying so I can better prepare your wardrobe and rations?"

"Not long. An Earth week, perhaps? That should be enough time to find what I need and travel back here in time to challenge Jaxson and the federation's board."

"My Queen, I am uncertain if a week of Earth's time will be enough."

"Doesn't their cycle work like ours?"

"No, it does not. Time is different there. It is hard for me to explain, but you will see a day pass with both light and dark. When it is dark, you will know that a day has passed, and little activity happens until the sun rises the next day. Their moon cycles take 30 days of light and dark."

"But it still sounds like it will take less than a cycle to gain someone with a viable seed."

"I'm sure you are right, my Queen. I will prepare your ship, but are you sure you don't want me to travel with you?"

Tilda brushed some loose strands of Verena's chestnut locks from Verena's cheek.

"You've grown up so fast and so strong, Verena. I understand you may not need me as much as you once did, but you can't blame me for wanting to come and help."

"Tilda," Verena started as she took Tilda's hand, cupping her cheek, and placed it in hers. "You have been the mother I haven't had for many years, and I can't thank you enough for your devotion and love. But I need you here for our planet in my absence. Even though the Valet de Chambre made Jaxson swear to a truce for this whole heir business, I do not trust that he will keep to that promise. Until I am with child, I wouldn't put it past him to attack in my absence. And it would break my heart, as it would yours, to come home to that kind of loss. Please see that our people are safe and continue to train for the next battle."

"Yes, your Majesty. I will."

Tilda bowed her head slightly and smiled as she cupped Verena's face once more.

"And please make sure that you come back to us safely. The Earthlings may be primitive, but that doesn't mean they are tame by any stretch of the means."

"I understand, Tilda."

ABOUT THE AUTHOR

USA Today Best Selling and award winning author Amanda Kimberley has written in various genres in the course of almost four decades.

Her nonfiction blog, which focuses on the chronic disease fibromyalgia, has garnered recognition from various organizations, including Health Magazine. Naming her blog, Fibro and Fabulous, as a top blog for fibro sufferers.

Amanda has also written for medical magazines

and sites like FM Aware, The National Fibromyalgia Association's magazine and ProHealth.

When Kimberley is not writing nonfiction, she enjoys penning romance. Her first Furry United Coalition story, The Turtle and the Hare, earned the 2020 Summer Splash Book Awards of Ink and Scratches for Best Romance. Her Forever Series Books, Forever Friends and Forever Bound were featured in 2015 and 2016 on the BookCountry website, a division of Penguin/Random House as editor's picks. She has also been featured as a USA Today Happy Ever After Hot List Indie Author with Claiming My Valentine, a Best Poet of the 90's ranking for an anthology, and has had a #1 PNR ranking with Immortal Hunger and Hearts Unleashed.

Amanda Kimberley is a Connecticut native that now lives in the warmth of Northern Texas with her zoo consisting of her husky, tuxedo cat, mice, rabbits, guinea pigs, a tank of fish, two daughters, and a husband.

When she is not writing you can find her cooking whole foods for her pack. She also enjoys reading, hiking, and gaming.

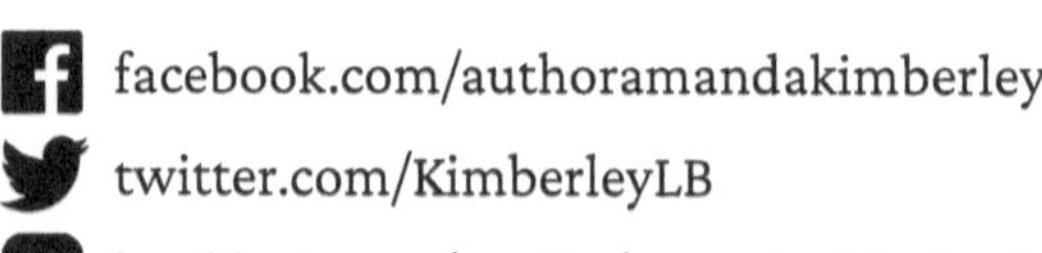

facebook.com/authoramandakimberley

twitter.com/KimberleyLB

bookbub.com/profile/amanda-kimberley

ALSO BY AMANDA KIMBERLEY

PNR Series

The Forever Series

Forever Friends

Forever Tied

Forever Cherished

Forever Bound

Forever Immortal

Forever Blood

(Coming Soon)

Forever Loved

(Coming Soon)

Forever Yours

(Coming Soon)

Forever Mine

(Coming Soon)

Historical PNR Series

The Witch Journals Series

Salem's Trial by Judge

Salem's Trial by Township

Salem's Trial by Birth

(Coming Soon)

The Gypsy Witch Trials

(Coming Soon)

Colonial Witch Trials

(Coming Soon)

Stand Alone PNR

The Cure

Manifestations

Uncharted

The Pride Within

(Coming Soon)

The Pandemic Series

Pandemic Passion

Pandemic Pandemonium

(Coming Soon)

The Midnight Rising Series

Midnight & Mistletoe

Midnight & Magic

(Coming Soon)

Midnight & Memories

(Coming Soon)

Midnight & Mergers

(Coming Soon)

RomCom PNR

The Eve L. Worlds Hellenic Island Shifter Series

The Turtle and the Hare

The Turtle and the Rock

The Ferret and the Fossa

The Leopard and the Llama

(Coming Soon)

Contemporary Romance

The Chronic Collection

Down by the Willow Tree

To Hell With Carpets

Welcome Home

The Chronic Collection

The Just Series

Just Breathe

Just Believe

(Coming Soon)

Just Be

(Coming Soon)

Nonfiction Self Help

The Fibro and Fabulous Series

Fibro and Fabulous: The Book

Fibromyalgia and Sex Can Be a Pain in the Neck

Fibromyalgia and Pregnancy

Poetry

Blue Water Baptism

The Puzzle Called Life

For More Information Please Visit: https://www.bookbub.com/profile/amanda-kimberley